BEYOND THE WALLS

Beyond the Walls

New Writing from York St John University

2019

Valley Press

First published in 2019 by Valley Press
Woodend, The Crescent, Scarborough, YO11 2PW
www.valleypressuk.com

ISBN 978-1-912436-29-3
Cat. no. VP0149

A CIP record for this book is available from the British Library.

Text design by Jamie McGarry.

Contents

Foreword, Dr Naomi Booth 8
Preface, Student Editorial Team 9

POETRY

Church Road, Plattsmouth, Nebraska, Colin Cutler 11
Not Ordinary, R.J. Brookes 12
Sonnet 130 (Revised): The Vanity of the Muse, Heather Lukins 13
Secret Lives Behind Uncanny Doors, Heather Lukins 14
The Lighthouse at Lindisfarne, Georgina Kerr 15
Reflection, Elizabeth Fitzgerald 16
Home, Aimée Donnell 17
Rumour Has It, Jennifer Keighley 19
After the Fall, Alice Leon 20
Mine NOT Yours!, Eleanor Hartley Smith 21
You make me hate walking, James Rance 22
Asian Ordination, Michael Donnelly 23
Old Lives, Stacy Curry 24
Grasp, Thomas Markham 25
That Horrid Place, Paul Whelan 26
Old Seas, Tom Young 27
Jane Doe, Georgia Fenwick 30
Defined (A Spoken Word Poem), Jessica Whittall 31
Home, Samantha Bland 32
Soaked, Kate Hewett 33
A Ruckus, Elizabeth Bell 37
Confidence, Grace Morris 38

NON-FICTION

The Mourning After, Caitlain Jayne Horan   39
Grandma's House, Imogen Peniston   41

FICTION

Light Beams, Matthew Pickering   43
The Land of Unbecoming, Amy Stewart   45
Tattoos, Tia Welsh   47
The Deal, Jackson Smith   48
The Viola Teacher, Kathryn Sharman   50
The Sum of Our Parts, Grace Cooper   54
CaRiCaTuRe, Aimée Donnell   56
This is who we are, David Yeomans   58
The Grimm, E.L. Thompson   60
BB and the Three Little Pigs, Hollie Glover   62
The King and The Stranger, Abbi Peace   64
Autumn Anne, Amy Craig   66
No, I Am Not, Andrew Milne   68
Love Letters, Abby Knowles   70
Commotion in the Corporation, Ben Ambrazaitis   73
Gunshot, Stacy Curry   75
String Making, Jamie-Louise Shakeshaft   76
Mr Smith, Vicky Booth   78
Death in New Orleans, Megan Tait-Davies   80
Bitter, Patrick Morgan   82
The Man Who Smiled, Joshua Liddle   85
Gas Leak, Grace Morris   87
Four Ghosts of Martin Croft, Neil James Hudson   89
Heat Death, John Liddle   92
Black Shuck, Charles Plumb   93
Eric's Flat, Jessica Wright   94

Foreword

It is a great pleasure to invite you to read and to celebrate the work collected in the *Beyond the Walls* anthology 2019. Each year we publish some of the very best new writing from our students at the York Centre for Writing at York St John University, and each year I am dazzled by the range and the brightness of their work. This year, the pieces take us from Yorkshire to Nebraska to Mars. This anthology appears at a time when what it means to be "at home" in a particular country, or "at home" in an uncertain world, is an urgent question for many. The work collected here shows that the next generation of writers are thinking about this with great energy and imagination. You'll find writing here that expresses love for particular places and for the idea of home; and writing that attempts to smash-up familiar and domestic imagery. You'll find writing that celebrates past traditions; and writing that defaces the past to make something new. You'll find grief and violence and nostalgia; and experimentation and wild humour and totally new horizons too.

With this anthology, we celebrate the achievements of the 2019 cohort of Creative Writing graduates, their hard-work and immense creativity. Our second-year students, as part of their Production, Publication and Performance module, have worked tirelessly to bring this anthology into being: they've read and edited and promoted the work of the writers included here, as well as selecting cover art from the talented artists at YSJU and organising a brilliant showcase as part for the York Literature Festival. They've been led in this task by the indefatigable and inspirational Dr Adelle Stripe, as well as working closely with our publishing partner, Valley Press. It has been our privilege at the York Centre for Writing to offer a home to the writers included here over the course of their degrees. The writing gathered in this anthology shows how ready they are to go out into the world, to make a home of it – and to change it too, with their courage and energy and vision of how things might be. In the words of Elizabeth Bell, one of the writers included here, I hope that all of them will make a ruckus in whatever way they can; and, when times are tough, that they remember the great power of their collective imaginations and to "be brave, be brave".

Dr Naomi Booth
Subject Director for Creative Writing

Preface

York is a city that is impossible to define. A city that contains Roman ruins, Viking remains, a Gothic cathedral and Victorian splendour crisscrossed with medieval cobbles; the identity of York is an ever-shifting thing. Likewise, nestled beyond the ancient walls, York St John University has an identity in flux. Starting life as a Victorian teacher training college to become a vibrant, tight-knit university community with a hotbed of creative talent, the students of York St John are just as in flux as the city. This anthology explores the multi-faceted question of identity, from what you are willing to give up to regional folklore. *Beyond the Walls 2019* moves beyond the walls of our city to look at who we are, what we believe in, and the things that scare us. Who will you become after venturing *Beyond the Walls*?

Student Editorial Team

2019 Editing Team

Jessica White, Amy Langton, Courtney Wakelin, Freya Bainbridge, Emily Hambley, Phoebe Robson, Sophie Kilmartin, Conor Hannon, Sarah Ikin, Bern J. Anderson, Kerri-Anne Lee, Ross Tandy, Maia Gunning, Emily Stone, Lucy Embleton, Lucy Appleyard

2019 Marketing Team

Erin Abrey, Keegan Grey, Ethan Newton-Hamer, Hannah Petch, Caroline Dinsdale, Anna Carroll, Cameron Law, Courtney Birks, Catherine Gent, Adlin Izat Amir, Charlotte Doyle, Alexandra Cousins

2019 Podcasting Team

Lewis Sayers, Elizabeth Carr, Jeremy Ceri Mitchell, Caitlin Fivash-Henderson, Jake Sherris, Rogan Phillips, Charles Hall

Church Road, Plattsmouth, Nebraska

I did not love you till
I read Willa Cather twice describe
your skies and fields as sheet-tin,
hard   brittle   rattling and gray as god
riding down from Canada
on the winter wind and
fraying corn-stalk fibers
until they split –
my skin split, too, like the glass in our front
door
and my joints turned ashen and they ached.

A mile away, across the Union Pacific line,
a creek, and up the slow slope
to Arlo Cole's seed farm,
was a telephone pole, tall and barren
as a roadside
Pentecostal cross.

we always had a snow just prior to Christmas,
and most years, an ice storm
that left the moonlit fields glowing
with the shattered glory of fallen starlight.

On New Year's Eve, I would walk that mile,
and then the second mile back,
to burn my lungs with the bone-dry air,
and burden it with clouds.

Colin Cutler

not ordinary

i now realise
that i was never
meant to be
ordinary

as my journey
isn't an ordinary
tale

R.J. Brookes

Sonnet 130 (Revised): The Vanity of the Muse

Each morning I wake and start my regime:
Smash! A crystal glass ruptures, shards scatter,
I place them in my sockets, my eyes gleam;
To make my lips now kissably fatter
Pluck! Two red petals I wear from a rose;
My thighs are cellulite maps, the skin dun,
My bathing of mule's milk I now disclose;
In heaps and bags, hay stuffing weighs a tonne,
I unzip my flesh and fill out my curves –
Arse, tits, a little less around my hips;
At last, I reach for the many white pearls
I stick them in my gum line, red blood drips.
      And yet, by God, this is your fantasy,
      What do you think, sweetheart, do you now love me?

Heather Lukins

Secret Lives Behind Uncanny Doors

███████ phantasmagoric. ████████████
█████████ n suburbs. █████████████████

████████████████████████████████████
████████████████████████████████████
████████████████████████████████████
██████████████████████████

███████████████████████████████████

█████████████████████████ that place where it is extremely difficult to
████████████████████████████████████
████████████████████████████████████

████████████████ 'take the housetops off . . . ' ████████████████
████████████████████████████████████
████████████████████████████████████

██████████████████████████████████ 'peep in
at the ███████████████████████████████
████████████████████████████████████
████████████████████████████████████
██████████████████

████████████████████████████████████
████████████████████████████████████
be like. If the suburb cannot be properly seen, known and represented
then we can at least re-present it by producing a show of handy suburban

████████████ melancholy, frustrated, petty, house-proud women,
with infantilised, incompetent and trapped men, su██████████████
████████████████████████████████████
████████████████████████████████████
suburban thinking, especially in the thirties, in his *The Intellectuals and
████████████████████████████████████

i███████████████████████████████████
████████████████████████████████████

'Is this London?'

████████████████████████████████████
████████████████████████████████████

Heather Lukins

The Lighthouse at Lindisfarne

I watched as they left me,
Rowing away from my island home.
Their boat tossed around in the storm,
Ripping a young girl away from the world.

My protector and his daughter,
Stranded out here to save the lives of others.
Ensuring the torch I bear burns bright through the dark,
Keeping travellers away from my rocky base.

A band of men were rescued from the waves,
By two people as adrift from the land as them.
Cut off by the unforgiving sea that surrounds me,
Which daily retreats to reveal a road of sand.

Now father and daughter have departed from this land,
Watching the Holy Island of Lindisfarne,
I will always stand.

Georgina Kerr

Reflection

Your reflection is not your own
it does not belong to you
You are a rock battered against sea cliffs
changing and moving with the tide
Your reflection is not your own
You are the stories told on paper
legends passed down through families;
scratching your throat like sandpaper
Your reflection is not your own
You are stone carved by mankind
moulded into the image of belief
a painting constructed from lies
Your reflection is not your own,
until you break the mirror

Elizabeth Fitzgerald

Home

One big step into an empty
Yellow corridor, with my hair tucked
Beneath the harness of bags which
Are all still laden with home.
There's a coldness to the
Shadows I pass, each one mimicking
Some form of the past as I mould myself
Into the foundations to leave my mark.
My mark. What is my mark?
Am I just a fingerprint smudge lost to
The abyss of time, or will I imprint
Upon the earth with my words
Like the roots of a tree?
But now half of my future is
Mapped out ahead of me
And I fumble to forget
The discarded versions of myself I
Once wired together with a
Paperclip and a pen.
There's new clouds in the sky
And those aren't the clouds that
I'm used to as nostalgia passes me by like
A fleeting, slightly uncomfortable pat
On the back. Neither reassuring nor inducing
Panic attacks as I start to unpack and
One by one, feel my body come undone
And lose some experience to
Kneeling on the carpeted floor.
Patience is detected in my father's preaching
As reality toys with my vulnerability. No more
Frequent offerings of warm mugs
Of tea, each one sighed but always made
For me in the comfort of my own home
Amidst tired family walls.

Lone mornings croon for the
Silence of coffee as I constantly
Feel for my phone in my pockets –
To keep the messages from you like a
Picture in a locket as I clatter
The silence like the ballet dance of ripples
On a lake by turning on
The TV. But then the dreaded news
Awakens me, and suddenly the
Absence is ringing in my bones as
Suddenly I realise that I am alone
And will need to carry through
What I wanted to do. Or perhaps
I will flee back to where I came
From to realign once more
Where our stories have been told.
Take myself back to where you are.
That's home.

Aimée Donnell

Rumour Has It

Rumour has it that I am dead,
With flowers placed above my head.
Quite untrue, of course: a lie!
I am not dead. I did not die.

I was only pretending to fall away
To be forgotten with each passing day
To ease your pain, oh dearest
Because to you I was the nearest –

And death would surely part us,
Oh, it feels only my right to fuss
You shall not cry in my name!
And I shall not lay you to blame!

Or blame those that stood between us boldly
Because I am sure they lie just as coldly
They are the men that say I am gone –
Do you believe them because it has been so long?

I cannot tell much from where we are apart
But if you are moving, then it is a start.
For though rumour has it I am no more,
I have but closed a window, and quietly let myself out the door.

Jennifer Keighley

After the Fall

Shadows walk here
Beneath the tracks
Like moving cracks
Why did I die?
    1) Broke my body
    2) Broke my mind
    3) The solution I couldn't find
Until
It was too late and
Part of me was always going to be
                    Broken
It's ok, though
I don't need all my parts
And the ones that are broken can be
                    Discarded
And replaced with other things
Things I wasn't born with
But will soon become me
And I'll be
                    Better
Dad, do you recognise me?
Mum, who do you see?
Because I don't know who I see
When I look at you
Did we ever know each other
Before?

[what before what]

                The fall

Alice Leon

Mine <u>NOT</u> yours!

"Sharing is caring" – a relatively accurate cliché.

Lesson 101: sharing equals friends.
Lesson 102: friends equals fun.
Lesson 103: fun equals injuries.
Lesson 104: injuries equals experience.

Lesson 105 untold: friends are for material things and emotional support only.
Lesson 106 untold: never take advantage of generosity.
Lesson 107 untold: wisdom does not come with age; it comes from decisions, mistakes and experience.
Lesson 108 untold: mistakes are repeated, for you fall more than once.

Lesson 109 screamed and shouted: my body is mine, not yours.
Lesson 110 shouted and ignored: my permission is needed before you touch me.
Lesson 111 ignored and disregarded: you do not have possession over me.
Lesson 112 disregarded and shouted: no means no.

Lesson 113 quiet and whispered: you can do this, show them you're strong.
Lesson 114 whispered and mumbled: you can't do that, it's not normal.
Lesson 115 mumbled and unheard: mental illness is caused by lack of voice.
Lesson 116 heard yet silent: I AM HUMAN!

Lesson 117 heard but not understood: respect of my body should be given unconditionally.
Lesson 117 part two heard but not understood: respect for each human is earned.

"Nothing is ever as it seems"   "Take nothing at face value"

You make me hate walking

I've said it a thousand times. you've heard it
a thousand through: this body is no longer my own.
it lies here paralysed, only saved from
sinking into the mattress by the breadcrumbs
that form a protective skin. still I break myself
over the stairs and scatter in gold paper
all across the house. Still I take in and release curses
and scatter dill-weed all across the house, while
I mediate or meditate or
            marinate in the off-white I leaked
day by day into the bedsheets, around in
front of me there extends a tree,
with new branches growing, emerging
with every unmoving choice I make.
As they widen and grow branches of their
own, few branches bear fruit
but many freeze and tumble to the ground,
the ends heal over and that space
will never feed anyone, merely serving
as an aching nub to be thought about
on the quiet days and the loud ones; I've
said it a thousand times:
this body is no longer my own.

James Rance

Asian Ordination

Gracious guardians of the pagoda prepared me.
Shaved my head and wrapped me in my saffron robe,
and I prostrated myself on the temples cool tiled floor.
Beneath the serene stare of a Buddha draped in gold.

Venerable monks repeated their rhythmic orations,
The Lord Buddha, The Dharma, The Monkhood,
Intoned in an ancient language their prayers resonated,
Sonorously, in the humid heavy, incense scented air.

White lotus blossoms floated on the blessed water,
that fell like spring showers on my freshly shaved skin.
Searching for tranquillity, love, and selflessness,
I laid thinking through a thousand mundane things.

Michael Donnelly

Old Lives

The shell that rots the souls
Who choose to stay
Is my cage no longer.
I have gone to better
things than that place
could offer. I have
want for better things
than that place could offer.
Toothless monsters with
tired dreams there is no
more threat of becoming.
Old lives, no longer relevant
only used to tell stories,
An example of what
should never be.
I am cleansed.
I am new.
I am free.

Stacy Curry

Grasp

Because if love is not
enough, why don't you
just let me go?
This is something I can't write

my way out from
I write
time and time
again
about my words
but they never affected you anyway.
Otherwise, you'd still be here
with me.

Thomas Markham

That Horrid Place

You're lying in bed, alone
Or with another person,
And you cannot stand
The thought that out there,
Through the walls,
Is where all the people are.

They use ovens, purchase clothes,
Go clubbing and vomit on your shoes.
They say things you cannot believe
And things that make you gasp.
They invite you places
You would never go
And, more often,
Places you would never go *with them*.

The people respire like you.
They are complex structures
Of bone, muscle, mucus, saliva.
Fundamentally:
Throbbing organs and
Gnashing teeth.

Paul Whelan

Old Seas

I am born
       on sapphire skin.
It laps at me
       softly. I am an
infant, afloat
       in the eye of
an asterism,
       balmed by
the rays of
       doubleblood
              days.

The weather unsettles. I am benighted. The surface breaks under my growing body and thunder shatters the tranquil air, booming in the ocean. The waves slap me down and submerge me. I open my eyes.

Baby blue
       decays. I
stretch out
       my legs and
flail for the
       black beds
          below.

The open water is a menagerie of monsters. Lithe krakens coil their oily limbs in the shade, as I sink into a space devoid of stars to mark or chart how far I have fallen into the dark.

I am
         suspended
amid
         megalodon
mouths
         baleful
smirks
         massive
                  faces.

Leviathans languidly unwrap their behemoth bodies and lour at
my floundering in the airless realm of tar. I crumble under the
deadweight of darkness. I tremble at the sinuous language of
wyrms resounding through the bowels of the world.

I am a
         drop of
blood
         sinking
slowly
         into a
hive of
         gods
that have
         not sated
                  for an age.

I'm woken by the cold in a trench at the core of the Earth and
I stand to look up to the surface so far above. I feel cleansed
by the saltwater, matured by the descent. I take my first step to
climb the continental shelf.

Each step
        I take
the higher
        I climb
the less
        I feel
                fear.

My ascension is calm. From here, the colossal squids and
spiders seem as still as weeds. I make my peace with these
old seas and stagger from the surf. The salt fizz peels from
my skin as I collapse on the beach.

Short years
        blow away
in a swift
        sea breeze
                and

my terrible ocean, boundless, bottomless and black, is gone.
Only now can I keen for my time in the dark deep as a shell
of bleached bone, stranded in the glare of immaculate sand.

Rot has
        washed out
all my
        old
flesh
        and
                pain.

Tom Young

Jane Doe

Silence surrounds you
watching
as you weave between
rows upon rows of
history, calling
to the land of the living.
Stone harsh to your touch,
a reminder of time passed,
meaningless dates and names,
caressing their words,
memory teasing your mind
as it slips from your fingertips
making you wonder
what could have been.

Georgia Fenwick

Defined (A Spoken Word Poem)

I am a woman and a writer,
a feminist and a survivor.
I am a warrior against a system that feeds
the excessive need for unjust greed.
Punk will never die, she screams.
                              Or at least that's what I try to be.
And when I think, what does identity mean to me?
I stumble and I stop.
The path is sharp and dour and means that I can't see
the positives, a conditioned aversion to confidence.

Now I know I am loyal and humble,
I'll give you the coat off my back if you need it,
                              and I have.
But then something gives,
and now loyalty feels like naïve stupidity,
someone will only take what they need,
                              and they have.
I have always sought out the light,
a pessimistic hedonist, from the red glow of cigarettes to bonfires on
    the beach.
I've fought the battles against the waves of dependency and won.
        I get head fucks about things like gender, and
                  if you don't, you don't know, you know?
                        But if I was given the choice to be sent back
                              and choose,
I'd be born a woman.
And that doesn't mean I don't think gender is oppressive and shit;
it just means that, on the road to its destruction,
I'll make it my weapon and I'll fight with it.
At twenty-eight I'm just learning to forgive myself,
how to say no and possess my own authenticity.
But who am I?   Who am I?

The fuck if I know.

Jess Whittall

Home

My fingertips ache with the touch of the familiar as I trail my hand across the branches. Every brush of contact between skin and the falling leaves reminds me that I am here. I am here again, and not in a dream. The weak blush of the early sunlight soaks my face as I tip my head back. I savour the sensation, and a sigh of contentment passes my lips. My eyes find the lake and fall upon the endless creases of the water, the movement of each ripple identical to the last but becoming impossibly more hypnotic with every new wave. I shiver, hugging my body close to escape from the threat of the strong breeze, to hide from the whistle of the wind. Comforted by the illusion of extra heat, I let the hazy nostalgic feeling of returning to my childhood home well up inside me. Without warning, the rain comes, but this time I willingly let it take me. I won't let my thoughts pale and darken at the promise of my limited time. Raising my arms, palms outstretched to the sky, I allow myself to feel every droplet before it falls and sinks. No, nothing can quench the happiness coursing through my veins. This is where I belong, and this is where I will remain until I am unable to remain any longer.

Samantha Bland

Soaked

as you lay

  i lay

down my head   and the rest of us follows

  you & i

    laying down

      where the sea meets the land

you flatten yourself into your sea bed

  in return i

    push into the sand   forsure   leaving an imprint   of my body

          we are

          full more with booze than blood

full to the brim it leaks out of

          you & i

            in furious undulations of nausea

the sea stings our lips   the small cuts   shouting   buzzing   from the salt

fret not

for the fish piss   you must be licking from your lips

your tongue is appeasing the salt

pleading   mercy   mercy   mercy
                              for spilt lips

i wonder

will anyone notice

us

lingering at the edge of this world
        will they come say hi
        will they come to ravish?
                you or i

you or i

non-yet

have ravished

I have

wet dreams of desire into stuffed toys

albeit this number is limited

of all the men I've known

whimper

secretly

and dissolving after lust fades

etches promising love

whispered into like youths

you & i

would Poseidon be different?

if he doesn't appear

you have been caressed

ears bearing small marks   gifts from clumsy canines

will lay here   fully soaked in salt and fish piss

waiting for the dawn

Kate Hewett

A Ruckus

"When I dare to be powerful, to use my strength in the service of
my vision, then it becomes less and less important whether I am afraid."
– Audre Lorde

This is not a poem for the child you were, nor the woman
you will one day become. It is a screaming resolution, an
aching promise to whichever beautiful and powerful role
you are playing today. To the woman whose skin may be
thick and calloused, or equally thin – cracked and chapped
and in need of healing. To the grazed knee, split gum, dark
eyed child you were, or
the loud-mouthed political teenager, calling me at midday
to tell me of the new evils of the world that lie under the
shadow of an old man's boot. Your face: chestnut in the
sun, so different from the startling paperwhite-to-lobster
shades of my own, pressed into my memory between two
pages, soaking up the seawater and tan on that secret beach,
claiming it our own. Or again, the wet-eyed look you gave
me, brave and bullied, bold and brilliant, toasting sugar-
pink marshmallows over the old gas hob. The day you
told me I was good at my job, the day I found pride in
how I had managed to get it right this time. The day you
scared the shit out of me, hitting the ground with your
soft cheeks, blood from your mouth shockingly red against
the blue of the tarmac, the first time I remember feeling
helpless, feeling responsible. This is not a poem for the
child you were, nor the woman you will one day become,
it is not a pretty thing, it is not a luxury. This is an oath to
every shadow and crease you have lived in, the corner of
the sandpit that you inhabited, the flesh and blood that
fuses us, the DNA we share, the memories we have survived
together. This is a call to arms. This is a riot, a ruckus, the
wild rumpus begins: to the child you were, to the woman you
will one day become, let every incarnation shout violently,
whisper quietly –
and be brave, be brave.

Elizabeth Bell

Confidence

Confidence is freedom.
Is trapping.
Is deafening.

Watching people with confidence is a trap.
They inspire you.
They scare you.
They own everything about themselves,
Or at least let you think they do.

They make you ask yourself.
What do I need to do
To be like them?
Almost every time the answer isn't accepting yourself,
It's fake it 'til you make it.

That phrase can be deafening,
It drowns out everything.
Until it doesn't.
You're left more scared of the world than you were before.

Don't let the fear stop you.
Sweaty palms,
Short breaths,
Heart beating so hard you think your ribs might crack.

All tricks to keep you trapped.
To keep you from telling the world a secret.
A secret few may know,
A secret that is nothing to be ashamed of.

A secret that owned,
Frees you.
Because confidence isn't something to be told.
Confidence is something to see.

Grace Morris

The Mourning After

At first my grief could not be explained, the insidious ache cleared the air from my lungs. Once I had attached the word 'grief' to this emotional parasite, I felt like I had crossed a line into a place I had no right to be. There was nothing for me to mourn. I had not lost anything or anyone. A single question remained; where had this anguish come from?

I conjured up the familiar images I usually associated with grief – a sea of black clothing, an almost endless river of tears, the irreversible stain of death. While I did tick a few of those I was still missing that key ingredient. The actual loss. Now, it seemed that this emotion had come out of nowhere. Yet, it was also eerily familiar. More like an old friend that had always been there, my constant companion.

It was when I was then asked about the odd label choice I had given that I realized just how stumped for an I answer I actually was. I had walked around so long with this grief wrapped tightly around my chest tumbled up in knots with no idea it was there at all. How was I now meant to identify something that had been so elusive to me?

Unravelling the thread was a painful process, the more we pulled and tugged at it the more stubbornly it would cling onto me in a refusal to tell the mysteries of my pain. Some days the result of the endless prying would leave it squeezing so uncomfortably on my heart as it pulled tighter, to the point that I swore I could feel it breaking under the pressure. It seemed that every time we pulled a knot free, three more would take its place, the longer this battle went on the less keen I was to keep tugging at them at all.

For a while my own deeply buried secrets kept their hold on me, then mercifully, I managed to cut it all loose.

That's when I realised this grief that I held wasn't grief in the conventional sense, but a pain born out of the loss for the young girl that I used to be. My teenager – I had been clinging firmly to her with everything in me even though she would not recognize me anymore. She had been dead for years and yet here I was still refusing to let her go. This girl that I knew was still with me every day, from the moment I woke up to the point I fell back to sleep.

I grieve for that girl who was constantly caught between two worlds, circumstance forcing her to grow up far too quickly and to carry so much weight on her tiny shoulders; weight that she wasn't ready to hold all up by herself. Thrown in at the deep end, she struggled to keep her head above the water while everyone around her seemed to be able to swim; they all paddled on by, ignoring her desperate pleas and leaving her stuck to learn alone. I grieve because that girl almost wasn't strong enough to keep treading water, to hold onto a life that barely felt like her own when she was so exhausted trying to keep it all up. She was so desperately alone and she doesn't know how to stop being alone now.

But mostly I grieve because I wasn't strong enough to save her and now, because of that she is lost to me forever.

Caitlain Jayne Horan

Grandma's House

My Grandma's kitchen smells like the deep fat fryer. The fryer sat on the counter is overseen by my Grandad who watches black and white war films in the kitchen with my brother. That's his room, decorated with family photos and porcelain horses working the land. The dogs live in his room too; generations of them have made their home in a bed next to the fire. This means that my mother will always strip us down and throw us in the bath as soon as we get home, covered in dog hair. As soon as we're home, all our clothes come off in the kitchen and go straight in the washing machine. My brother and I are forced to run through the house naked, straight into a red-hot bath.

There's a door that leads to the front garden, where the coal house is, one that leads to the back, and a jauntily placed door that leads to the garage. My grandad built the garage himself. That's where he keeps his car, one that you need a step to climb into. It's a Japanese import, even the numbers on the speedometer are Japanese characters and it has two tiny TV screens in the back which nobody knew how to use. The back garden was the best thing to ever happen to any child ever; it has a huge tree, swings, a slide and plenty of space to chase dogs around.

Grandma's room is the living room. Her corner sofa stretches the length of the room, no animal or dirty shoes dare to go near it. She always has a jigsaw, four or five real life magazines, and a cup of coffee on her collapsible dinner table. Her crystal ashtray used to stand on a pillar close beside her. She collects statues of African women in their native dress. These line her walls along with a display cabinet dedicated to our school photos which eventually over-spilling onto the floor and into Grandad's room (he has no choice). I like helping with the jigsaw, even though they frustrate me.

Grandma is a gem. She gets kookier and more aggressive the older she gets; every time I see her, she has a story to tell about her fighting someone in Greggs or having an argument with someone else from the village. My favourite story took place in Woolworths way back when my Mum was eight. The fabric counter lady was sniggering at my Grandma's hair which was backcombed to oblivion into a rugby ball shape – I'm sure it was the fashion in the 70s. Her response was unforgettable; she dragged the woman over the counter by her neck and whispered quiet threats to her. Nobody insulted her hair again and she remained as proud as ever.

Grandad's attitude was no better, of course. I've never seen anything but a soft old man with gelled back hair and a wispy beard. But, in his youth, he was famous in the village for looking strikingly like the Strongman Geoff Capes. He acted like him too, notoriously getting into a fight the night before his wedding, posing with a broken nose and a black eye in all the photos. A typical village boy, sticking up for his own no matter the consequences. Oddly enough, my fondest memory of my Grandad takes place early in the morning in a grotty charity shop. I pick up *An American Tail* from a box of assorted videos and offer it to him –

'Pass us your glasses, Sandra,' he grumbles.

'You've got your own!' She replies, handing them over to him anyway. Her glasses are huge, round and soften his hardened face as he studies the back of the video case.

We go back to her house in Grandad's monster car, excited about our new video. The car turns onto the street behind their house, facing the old quarry. Grandma jumps out to go through the front door, to unlock everything and check on the dogs. My brother and I always stay in the car, to help Grandad with the gate. We unlock the door that connects the garage and the rest of the house; the dogs come rushing through our legs, jumping at our feet. They continue to run between Grandad, Keir and I, as excited to see us as I was to be there.

Grandma has the video already set up when I get into her living room, there's always something on her tv because it's her pride and joy, the biggest flat screen on the market. I sit next to her, greasy chicken and chips on my lap, and through her perm she asks,

'Cartoons?'

Imogen Peniston

Light Beams

'Alright, Wes, put the headpiece on and close your eyes,' the doctor told me. 'It'll take you to a new location and we'll judge where you're most suited to work from there.'

'Where else have people been?' I asked. Candidates weren't allowed to talk to each other about their Trip. I think that the doctors were worried that it might scare people off if they knew what happened next.

'Our first candidate went to an island community that travelled across the ocean on a constant cycle. The second went to a world where all the oceans were acidic,' the doctor said, moving over to her monitor. 'But it's different for everyone, so we can't be sure where you'll end up.' She began typing. 'When you close your eyes, you'll see a white light that should last thirty seconds. Your vision should then adjust and you'll see where you are. Now, we're ready when you are.'

It was like a lamp being shone in my face. All colour drained.

My boyfriend took my hand and led me into the fog. Then he let me go before letting go and dissolving away from me. I couldn't smell anything, but every time I inhaled, I could feel the fog entering my body. I knew that I didn't have long before it consumed my body like it did his. I desperately hoped it was the fog of Silent Hill, because I at least could make my way through that.

I continued on from the spot he left me. There was tarmac underfoot and I could see the white lines of the road stretch on before me. I'd lost my shoes at some point. I had the distinct feeling that I had done something with them, but could not recall what. My boyfriend threw his in a river and they were carried away, I could piece that together, but not where mine went. This wasn't even real. In reality, I still had my shoes on, so where did I lose them?

A weapon was high up on my list of things to find, then shoes. How else do you survive Silent Hill?

There was a vaguely round, red flickering light appeared off in the distance. I could hear water running. With a few more steps I was on a bridge. A quick look over the side, you never know what'll you'll find – and a pair of shoes, pulled along by the current. *There they go. I bet he'd want them back, but I don't trust that I'd survive the drop.* Too late to act, the shoes disappeared under the bridge and into the fog as I continued to walk.

Towards the light was the only route that made sense. I know a light is what people see when they are close to death – and maybe I was. Maybe it wasn't a traffic light flashing. Maybe it was an angler fish with the muscular legs of my boyfriend, standing there with an axe, ready to hack me down. Or maybe it was neither of those.

Maybe it was the neon sign attached to a wall that it actually was. The sign that read 'Club 96'.

Inhale. The fog coated a lung.

Exhale. A door formed under the sign.

All logic suggested that a person shouldn't go in the room, but as my body filled with the fog, and with no other options – I had to.

'Did you see my shoes in the river?'

My eyes needed a break, the light was changing too much. And it didn't stop. A spotlight appeared and showed me a featureless figure – like one you'd see on a bathroom door.

'Isaac?' Fog streamed from my mouth as I spoke. The figure vanished and the fingers of my right hand interlocked with someone else's. They were Isaac's. 'Where am I?" Only his face was visible. A little of his golden fringe had fallen on his forehead.

'I don't know.' His face was soft. With each word, a little more of his body appeared in place of the grey figure.

'Alright, what happened to my shoes?'

'You don't remember?' I shook my head. His shoulders and arms appeared. 'You threw them up in a tree because I said I'd kiss you if you did.' He turned his head forward, "look there," and pointed with his free hand. His legs had appeared. He was completely with me.

I turned to where he pointed. A glowing green sign was before us.

'Who are you going to be, Wesley?'

'One vision is going to decide my entire future once I touch that sign, isn't it?' I asked, taking one last look at him. He squeezed my hand as I reached out to touch it.

The fog entered the room. It inched up my feet, around my body, my head. The two of us separating through beams of light.

My fingers gripped onto the sign.

Matthew Pickering

The Land of Unbecoming

How did you get here?

How did you find us?

No matter. Calm down. You're here now.

I'm going to tell you how to survive, because, quite frankly, I don't have time to bury any more bodies.

You see that lake, there? It isn't like any lake you might have seen before. There's a reason the surface is thick and soupy; a reason why you can't see the bottom. You can't go kayaking on it or dip your toes in or even splash your face on a warm afternoon. Why? Because something lives in that teal water. Some*one*. And to make a home here, to survive the disease beyond our borders, you must submit to her completely. You must give yourself to her, piece by piece. Only then will she protect you.

On the first Sunday of the month, at 2:58am precisely, everyone in this place walks down to the shore. We are grave about it – the occasion demands solemnity. Lanterns swing between us in the dark haw. Twigs crack underfoot. We don't speak – we don't wake her, if we don't have to.

We stop where the pebbles are damp and place our lanterns down. Everyone in turn, whether they're a day old or a day from death, makes a sacrifice. If we want her protection, we must feed her, and she won't accept any old thing. Every single item we send sailing into the lake has to have great significance to us personally. We give up chunks of ourselves.

Now, I know why you're wearing that expression. You're thinking, eventually, there must be nothing left to give? Well, you'd be right.

Here's a drink. I suggest you take a sip before I tell you the rest.

When physical things run out, you have to give parts of yourself. Secrets, desires, dreams. You bend down and you whisper them to the water. As she takes, you forget. She likes you to be blank, you see – she wants us all the same.

There are people here, the oldest of our residents, who've given up so much that they barely have any memories at all. I don't know where their minds go when they sit back in their rocking chairs. They don't have a selfhood – she's taken it. We'll all end up like that, one day. It's the price we pay to stay alive.

Oh, and don't even think about lying. Why? Because it happened once. Someone lied.

His name was Jonas. He was new here, just like you. He'd heard about the protection that she can offer. Heard that you're untouchable once you live here, that you're kept pure and humble. Like all of us, he gave what he could at the monthly ceremony. Sent photographs, clothing and letters down into the lake and into her dark belly. He lived with the barest of essentials, nothing which meant much to him. So, what else could he give?

Drink up, will you? It gets worse. Of course, it gets worse.

He spilled his secrets. Of how he'd been unfaithful to his wife, stolen a small sum of money from his brother. How he'd told his parents he'd gone to fight the disease – but really he was here, seeking protection. He became thinner and thinner – not particularly in stature, but just in *feeling* – we all go through that phase. We feel as if one gust of wind could send us dispersing into the atmosphere like a dandelion. After all, our secret desires and experiences are the threads that keep us all tightly stitched together. When they loosen, when she takes them – we begin to fade.

Jonas resisted it. The next giving ceremony, he told her a lie. He said that he drank too much when he'd never touched a drop. And she knew. There was trembling in the centre of the lake, as if someone had dropped in a pebble from high above. The circles rippled outward and began to spin, the water churning and churning – a violent maelstrom. The sound was the worst part, a kind of gelatinous sucking. I've since learned what it means, that wild call for blood. Lies are paid for in flesh. Jonas walked into the lake, and she took him.

Here's another drink. Take it easy, now.

The first ceremony is two days away. Once you start feeding her, you can't stop. But you still have time. You can give yourself up to her and stay alive, or you can stay who you are and take your chances out there.

So, what will it be?

Amy Stewart

Tattoos

You watch her through the window, dented with the remains of raindrops, picking at the scabs. They're soft and brown and wrinkled, like chocolate flakes. Mine are crispier. I know my future. She doesn't. Do you want to know? Always. She pauses to glance at you. Stop, I say. She does not stop. She is not your prisoner. *I am.* She is an artist. She shakes her head at you and carries on picking away with the knife. Picking, picking, picking. I like knives. Because you think picking away your problems is good, she whispers as the tears on my face start to fall. I want her to stop: you want her to keep going. She likes to draw, on her skin especially. The blood is my paint and the skin is her canvas. It's ugly artwork. Artwork that hums and drips with the power to cure. Perhaps it will cure you and me? Or perhaps it will shatter us all into a million tiny pieces?

Tia Welsh

The Deal

I looked in the mirror and my face stared back at me. Only, it wasn't my face, or at least not just my face. There was another image, imposed over the one in the mirror, they were swapping, flickering, merging into one another.

My face, my true face, shone through. Nobody else could see it. Maybe nobody would ever see it except for me. The expression it wore, that I wore, was one of pain and frustration. The other face, the one the world saw, the one that I stole… that one held a look of madness. It was screaming, always screaming and pleading and begging. There were marks on that phantom face where it had tried to scrape and tear away its flesh. Of course, he couldn't tear the real flesh; his flesh, my flesh.

Why are you doing this? The other face asked, screeching in the way it always did.

'I'm not doing anything,' I tell it, 'I don't know why this is happening.'

This is a lie. I know what's happening. At least, I think I do. The old proverb tells us to never make a deal with the Devil. Sounds easy enough, but they make such promises. It came to me at the crossroads, told me it could make me rich, successful, beautiful. It did more than just tell me, it showed me and when you see the kind of life you can have, what it can offer you… It's hard to resist.

You stole my face. You stole my body. You stole my life!

'I didn't know. I couldn't have known what it was going to do.'

I could feel the other face trying to pull away, to make me move, to take control. But t couldn't. It couldn't move me, just as I couldn't silence it. It had begun to scream again. Once it started screaming, it didn't stop for hours. I couldn't stop it, I couldn't block it out. So, I joined it.

The voice within and the voice without screamed together. We screamed at each other, we screamed at the world, we screamed and cursed at the one who put us together, locked in torment.

It's a strange thing to take over someone's life, to become somebody else. Physically, I'm completely different; different face, different body, longer limbs. My hair is a different shape, different colour; even the eyes are different, foreign. To be foreign, a stranger in the body that you're using… It's not right. It's not what I wanted.

'Oh, but it is.' He was here. The demon, the Devil, the one who tied us together. His voice was smooth like aged whiskey and he brought with him the smell of fresh, expensive cigar smoke. He looked like a salesman, with his slick suit and groomed hair. The only thing that gave away his true nature were his eyes: black, totally and completely black.

'You know, I don't understand this screaming, my friend. You wanted to be better than you were, to be somebody rich and important. Aren't you rich and important now?'

'You lied! You didn't change me, you put me in this,' I gestured into the mirror and saw the other face staring at the demon in fury, 'You killed me. My friends, they don't know me. And I don't know this bodies friends. I'm alone. Alone except for him.'

He laughed, 'But you are rich, no? Rich, famous, important, successful.'

'No! I'm not, this guy is! And he won't stop screaming!' I punched the mirror in frustration. The demon didn't even flinch. He just smirked.

Kill him.

'But you are him now. His body is yours, his reputation, his money, all yours.'

'It isn't mine. Not really.'

Kill him now.

The other face had fallen quiet… In the shattered reflection I saw him still staring at the demon and I could feel him trying to reach for a shard. I held him back for a moment.

'Can you fix this? Make things back the way they were?'

'The way I see it, there's nothing to fix.'

I nodded and for the first time stopped fighting the other face. We took a shard of the mirror and together we lunged, plunging it into his throat. He didn't react. He looked amused, curious. No blood spurted out of the wound, not even a gentle trickle slid down his neck.

The screaming started again.

'There is a way out,' he said, pulling the glass from his throat, 'there is always a way out.' He placed the shard in my hand, and smirked at me, as if he knew.

Do it. Just do it.

'It's nice to agree on something for once.' I said, as we drew the blade upon our wrists.

Jackson Smith

49

The Viola Teacher

She had tried to learn the viola herself once, as a child, in school; badly. The option of violin had been snapped up quickly by keener and presumably more knowledgeable parents, leaving her with its larger, deeper, less sexy cousin. When her daughter had shown her the letter from school, it was like a taunting telegram from the past: so much has changed since you were a child and yet nothing has changed at all. As the note passed to her hand, it felt like a paper gauntlet. Why this one, of all the many others, she had no idea. But encouraging Ellie to take up the instrument, willing her to succeed at it, suddenly seemed important.

That night, over cold pasta sauce on plates like a child's first painting, she'd broached it with Michael.

'Fine by me,' had been his usual response.

'But they're only offering viola. Wouldn't the violin be better?'

Frowning, a ghost of a smirk on his face: 'It's all scratching really isn't it?'

So viola it was. And that's how Mark Taylor came to be in their lives. Recently graduated, able to travel, reasonably priced, he was still hoping to 'pursue my own composition work when I –' but for now, tutoring would pay the bills.

'At least he's cheap,' said Michael.

'He won an award apparently,' she countered. 'Maybe we should offer him more?' Again, the frown, the amused shake of the head.

Tuesday afternoons soon became a small beacon in the week. At first she would check herself in the mirror. Once she added lipstick before opening the door. The time she found herself changing her outfit entirely, she knew the game was up. He always looked the same: t-shirt, jeans, trainers. His clothes were often crumpled but clean. He clearly didn't possess an iron. And, somewhat bizarrely, he carried a beaten-up leather briefcase. She imagined it to be filled with sheet music, stubby pencils, perhaps an apple slowly growing wizened. On the occasion he once wore a shirt – 'I'm meeting some friends later at a recital' – she felt a bolt of jealousy so strong, it made her grip the door handle to steady herself.

To begin with, he would quickly usher himself into the back room, an offer of tea politely refused. But the door was always left open of course. You have to in this day and age. She would listen to the rise and fall of his voice, buffered through the kitchen wall. Occasionally he would laugh good-naturedly as Ellie's bow sawed hoarsely back and forth. For many weeks, she was quite happily comforted by the repetitive plink-plunk of resonating strings. She liked the way he said 'pizzicato' and 'gooood', stretching out the word like a piece of bubble gum. They were steadily working their way through *Viola Debut: 12 Easy Pieces for Beginners,* the names of which – *From a Bridge, Howdy Pardner* and *Southern Fried Boogie* – had made Michael snigger, as he'd flicked through the slim, glossy booklet one evening.

And then, more often, she found herself leaning against the door frame, observing across the distance of the hallway, as he explained a phrase or, taking the viola from Ellie, demonstrated the correct positioning. She noticed the bitten nails and tobacco stains as his hands splayed and danced on wire. Dirty fingers doing beautiful things, she thought. One day he glanced over, conscious of being watched, and smiled. Another day, when Ellie had nipped to the loo, he'd wandered into the kitchen, commenting on a favourable cooking smell. Even then she knew it was a hackneyed line as she shrugged away that evening's meal. On the doorstep, he'd been distracted by a photo on the wall, reminiscing about how he holidayed in the same place when he was a kid. So by the time they'd reached *Air on a D String,* he'd already inserted his hand inside her bra. Caught in the limbo of the porch one night, the inner door not quite closed, the outer one not yet open, she stood there while long, lean digits, trained to extend beyond their natural reach, undid the buttons of her blouse. Beautiful fingers doing dirty things.

On that particular morning, she was lying in bed with Mark, breathing in whorls of smoke already processed once by his lungs. Yet again she idly wondered at the complacency of a husband who'd be duped by an open window and some air freshener. She was expecting a delivery but when the doorbell rang she still jumped. Winding herself into her dressing gown – an expensive kimono style thing she'd bought when Mark and she had first started sleeping together – she stumbled along the hall to answer it. In her peripheral vision was the omnipresent detritus on the hall table; school notices, a couple of borrowed books, sunglasses, keys. It bothered her but not enough to ever tidy it.

She was conscious of the finite patience most postmen are imbued with these days and lurched forwards. Vaguely registering the irritation of coir matting under her bare feet, she opened the door. Michael stared back at her, a mixture of exasperation and apology on his face. Books, school notes, sunglasses… and keys.

'Forgotten my bloody keys,' he said unnecessarily.

Why else would he be knocking on his own front door? Michael was often stating the obvious. "That cobweb's been there for ages." "This ham is out of date."

Except the forsaken keys hadn't been obvious to her that morning. She gawped at him wordlessly. Small patches of pink were blooming across his cheeks like paint in water and a light sheen of sweat basted his hairline and upper lip. Was he out of breath from running back to the house or just het up and cross with himself? Both, she imagined. He'd been gone well over an hour, more perhaps. Her mind was frantically cycling back over the events of the morning trying to visualise an imaginary clock and where its hands would now be located.

'I'm going to be back late tonight remember,' he said, pushing past her and into the hallway, snatching at his keys, scraping them across the surface before depositing them in his trouser pocket where they bulged like a fist. He paused briefly on the threshold and planted a kiss that missed her mouth but didn't quite make it to her cheek. He'd had a coffee already, she noted, as her nose curled.

'Sorry, got to go, late. Don't wait up,' he threw back and slammed the door behind him. He hadn't even asked why she wasn't dressed yet.

She paused in the hall, waiting for the blood to slow a little, staring at her pale feet, the painted toenails livid against the blueish tinge of her skin. Stepping back, as though measuring her pace in reverse, she glanced in the hallway mirror at the smeared makeup (too much, too early for a Wednesday). She looked like a white suburban geisha.

By the time she'd made it back to the bedroom, Mark was already dressed, apart from his feet of course. He seemed to have the same disdain for socks she'd witnessed in her children when they were little.

'Listen, this is not –' he began. 'I mean, that was a bit close, yeah? I don't think we should…'

'Calm down, it's fine, he's gone, it's nothing.' Her hands patted the air between them, like a conductor hushing an orchestra.

'Yeah but what if –?'

'He didn't.'

'But he could have done.'

She sighed impatiently.

'What are you doing?'

'I've got to go,' he said, casting around, looking for his trainers.

'No you don't.'

She was struggling to keep the sing-song in her voice. For the first time since she returned to the room, his eyes met hers and his movements slowed.

She was aware of the bright morning sunshine as it streamed through the curtains, exposing every line, every pore and turned away. Her hand rose to the back of her head, ruffled her hair before coming to rest across her face, her fingers creating a makeshift veil. She smiled up at him through it. He had known her just long enough to begin to recognise it as one of her tics.

'I have to…' he gestured towards the door.

'Fine, off you go then,' her voice tight and high this time.

She stepped back, clumsily throwing her weight against the wall while her other arm outstretched a doorman's welcome. He ducked his head needlessly as he crossed the threshold.

She watched his retreating back, heard the quick shuffle of jeans as feet found stairs. A pause. She pictured him sitting on the bottom step pulling on trainers, the laces never undone or redone but fixed in an enduring double knot. Within the folds of those knots would be fabric still a virgin white, as pure as the day they were first tied while all around them was now grubbiness, worn and grey. At face value they looked fine but to undo them now would reveal the batik-like contrast. Sometimes you can only appreciate how filthy something has become by seeing how clean it once was.

Kathryn Sharman

The Sum of Our Parts

The parts of the sum can be detached and reattached with almost no restrictions bar those that dictate human from animal. It is impossible to attach a leg where an arm could be, nor a face where the knee should be. There is room to add a little extra – a finger here, a toe there, but nothing as excessive as genitalia – but this trend quickly fell out of favour as the need to maintain balance won out. Lacking is a feeling all are familiar with. It begins in their youth, with the careless discarding of undesirable parts in a fit of teenage rebellion, believing that throwing out their selves is a skin-deep quick fix for a dissatisfaction that runs deeper than the body. Rare is the sight of a teenager with a complete set.

It is even rarer to find adults satisfied with their lot. Resigned to the unending nature of this internal war, they make do with what little they can get their hands on. At twenty, the ideal self is still an achievable fantasy. By forty, it's all but a forgotten dream, crushed not by a lack of desire but by a cruel financial reality. They make do, living their lives and getting by on a meagre income, but they still want. They still dream for the ideal nose, for scar-less arms, for a face free of wrinkles and for that rare natural blonde hair. They will swap with their friends for the figure to make them look good in that dress for the first time in years. They will all share that pair of knees that don't ache after a thirteen-hour shift. And they will pretend it is enough.

Even rarer still is the belief that parts are willingly and freely shared. With a loaned set of straight teeth comes the dark desire to keep them. And with a set of crooked teeth comes the blind, desperate need to take another's. The deprived still have a chance at bartering for their comfort – through an official trade that remains innocent only on the surface. No one cares that it is caked in filth and corruption: stolen parts, fraudulent deals, and dirty money. So long as they don't see the mud, they can live their lives walking on linoleum.

In our youth, wearing fine parts comes with the comforting knowledge of total social conformity. As an adult, wearing fine parts paints a target on your back. You learn to look over your shoulder at all times of the day, not to stand out. You learn to keep your best parts hidden, even in the sanctity of your own home. Looking good becomes a dangerous and selfish novelty. Whether from first-hand experience or from second-hand stories, you'll soon become acquainted with the very real fear of having your parts stolen by those who only value parts for their financial value.

The only way to truly protect yourself is to wear the undesirable parts of the unfortunate. The face riddled with scars, the eyes that no longer see, the leg that lacks its lower half. The rotting and moulding. The painful and aching. These are the parts you see in the streets. The only parts that are safe. But at what point – you wonder – does the need to survive overtake the need to impress? At what point can your parts make you desirable rather than easy prey? Being undesirable becomes the attractive option. Where exists this middle ground of true safety? Eventually, the only solution left is to withdraw from the world, away from the predatory eye of the public that only seeks to cause you harm. It's a fraction safer for those who long for the unworn parts of those who have never seen the cruel labour of a day's work, at the cost of caging yourself like a collection of exotic trinkets on display.

Always the parts, never the body. Never the whole, but just the sum of our parts. Reduced to walking products, commodities graded on efficiency and desirability. The self is traded off, another cheap and meaningless component among thousands. We become lost within our limbs.

Grace Cooper

CaRiCaTuRe

Colours clung to the air like fireflies fading out upon the delicate span of a spider's web. Hues of powdered oranges, silken indigos and marigold yellows throbbed in the evening dusk as the chaotic bustling of the circus' atmosphere escalated. Annabelle thought it was almost dream-like as she waded through the mass of swarming crowds, peaking with the high-pitched shrieks of excitable children. She wasn't sure of how she had got there. Her last memory was locking up her flat to pick up some milk from the corner shop. She was sure that she had not ventured much further than normal. Her head felt foggy. It was as if the inside of her skull had suddenly been inflated like a hot air balloon and was levitating somewhere between the clouds. Her body felt weightless as she brushed against straying limbs unsure exactly of where she was heading. Floating through the madness, she observed a line of children eagerly watching an elderly man weave cotton candy for their pleasure. Inside large metal cages there were lions with marvellous haloed mains and tigers with stark stripes passively pacing backwards and forwards. In fact, she was sure that upon her passing, these beasts positively purred.

'Excuse me?' Somebody tapped her shoulder. Annabelle turned and the person immediately stooped over low into a genteel bow. A long black tail-coat framed his appearance with a thin top hat upon his head. A pair of white gloves sheathed his hands smartly, clashing with the blood-red cravat puffing out from the collar of his shirt like a flamboyant robin's breast. He introduced himself as the ring master and claimed to have noticed Annabelle looking quite lost and in need of a friend amidst his display. Immediately, Annabelle could feel this pale-faced man with the thinly pointed nose seizing hold of her trust as a warm fizz aroused inside of her. Go with him. When the ring master happened to offer her refuge in the 'top tent' in which he resided, Annabelle felt herself respond automatically and followed him up through a deserted path she had previously neglected.

How strange.

They entered the crimson drapes of the tallest tent.

'Tea?' The ring master asked.

'Oh, yes please.'

As he drifted off to attend to the task, Annabelle stared all around her, drinking in the sights. The light inside the ring master's tent was tinted in scarlet reds, making her surroundings hazy and warm. Above her, squawking birds of fantastic exotic colours aerobated down from the canvas roof in golden cages. Somewhere nearby she could hear the faint and cosy cracklings of a subdued fire. But before she could raise the question of why a fire was blazing inside a tent, she caught sight of a large portrait in an ornate brass frame upon a wall. The picture was eden-esque, adorned with delicate white lilies and feathered with bushy greenery. Yet, the girl in the centre caught her attention most. She was slim, with bright red hair rippling over her shoulders and wore a plain white dress. Following its renaissance style, the girl stood upon bare feet. But what was oddest of all, was that chained to the girl's flowing locks was a round white dove. Annabelle touched her own hair. It, too, was the colour of fire. Her thoughts were interrupted by the ring master's return. He sat opposite her with tea for himself. The beverages sat inside dainty little china cups perched upon matching saucers.

'Have a sip,' he leaned in with a smile. 'It's my own calming recipe. Should ease some confusion I sense you're having.'

'How do you know what I'm feeling?'

The ring master grinned. 'Let's call it intuition. I feel I have a connection with you.' He took a sip.

Annabelle looked down at her own cup, which was releasing tendrils of thick lilac steam out into the air. With one look at the ring master, she felt encouraged and sipped at the hot liquid.

Then, everything flashed before her.

A distorted, fragmented laugh drunkenly spilled into her ears.

She felt herself fall.

Slowly opening her eyes, Annabelle stared up into the horizontal pattern of silver bars. She was no longer in the tent, but in a cage! She tried to jump to her feet but screamed instead as something pulled at the hairs on her head. She froze. The ring master approached the outside of her cage, a smile tugging at his lips.

'Have a look at yourself, my dear,' he mused, placing a hand-held mirror up against the bars. 'See how special you have become.'

Annabelle looked at her reflection. There was a frantic dove chained to her head.

Aimée Donnell

57

This is who we are

The Martian City Mound looks like a small, red conical termite hill, just half a metre tall, with a Mount Fuji cap of bright white carbon dioxide frost evaporating off the top into the warming morning air.

Johnny found the City Mound while out prospecting and he made first contact using the required FC protocols: Friendly stance. Cautious approach – and stick to the script when it comes to saying anything about humans or Earth. In other words, say nothing about humans or Earth. We don't want to prompt a War of the Worlds invasion, do we? Johnny transmitted the standard greeting in fourteen dead Martian languages over the intercom on his Do-all. 'On behalf of Mars Base, Hello! We are pleased to meet you.'

The little Martian critters swarmed over the Mound and milled about in panic. They didn't respond to Johnny's greeting, so he started up the language investigation program on his Do-all and left it by the City Mound overnight to discover the linguistics these little guys use to communicate. Each Mound is different. The Do-all relayed its telemetry back to Base this morning and Johnny sent me out to retrieve it.

To walk off-Base in the light Mars gravity is a treat. The exercise keeps my modified bones strong and it's refreshing to expose my pachyderm skin to the chilly Martian air. I carry a big shovel on my shoulder. It rests neatly between two of my four vertical breathing vanes, the huge pointed plates grafted onto my back that function as external lungs. They reach out and synthesize oxygen from the threadbare carbon dioxide atmosphere this cold planet wears as a scarf. As I lope across the red dusty ground toward the Martians' little stronghold, the breathing plates bounce tightly up and down, pulling skin. My footprints press deep into the Martian sand.

Back on Earth, they call us Stegs, after the stegosaurus, or 'flies. Neither name is flattering, though a butterfly is a prettier, if more misleading description. Our insulated skin is so thick and heavy that even if we had muscles to beat our bony respiratory wings, we could not soar above the red dirt of our new home. We can never return to our first planet. Reconversions to Earth-normal bodies are expensive and risky, and they wouldn't want us back as we are. Earth is finished with dinosaurs.

So what did the Martians have to say when the language program did its thing? Same as always, 'Kill the intruders! Ready the Mound for war!'

When I arrive at the Martian City Mound, I can't help but laugh. It's so small! Only sixty centimetres in diameter. A dark line of miniature vehicles is winding out from a hole in the bottom of the hill. A microscopic rocket shoots up from the convoy and detonates across my thick leg with a dull crackle. Then a salvo of missiles crashes against my shin. Ow! It prickles!

Bellowing, I raise the shovel over my head and bring the blade down flat on the Martian procession. One slap is enough to beat the whole military cavalcade into the ground. Dust billows out from the impact, overwhelms my throat filters and I am coughing uncontrollably. Martian dust is glassy sharp and tastes of blood. Half blinded, I excavate the Mound, digging down into the gritty soil for nearly half a metre. I pour warmed sulphuric acid into the remains, to exterminate any survivors. Not exactly First Contact compliant, but hey, we have to live here.

That's my job done for the morning. I rub my throat, which will be raw for days, and shrug my shoulders to shake off the ice that has gathered on my breathing plates. There's an acid splash on the front panel of Johnny's Do-all and he won't be best pleased.

David Yeomans

The Grimm

They used to make sure the first body buried in a new graveyard was a dog. My grandma told me this when I was a little girl. They buried the dog and its spirit would stay in the graveyard as a guardian. It would prowl between the tombstones and keep the evil things out. Sometimes, if you were unlucky, you might see the dog prowling and then death wouldn't be long in coming for you.

Today they buried a young woman. I stand over her grave, my feet planted in the fresh turned mud, facing the gateway of the graveyard. Beyond, the dark things lurk. I see them in the flicker of movement at the edge of my vision, the darting of a shadow between two branches, the pooling of darkness like thick treacle in the cracks in the pavements.

A dog is a good guardian. It's fast. Vicious when needed, and deeply loyal. I can see why they would want a dog to guard the graveyard.

A fragment of a shadow breaks off and rushes towards the gate, turning and circling back at the last second. Below me, the first wispy strands of the girl's spirit start to emerge. She's fog rising from the earth, already beginning to lose her shape. Her lips curl at the edges with eyes, closed in sleep, that are more a suggestion than anything, an interplay of swirling vapour.

I used to believe in heaven. I used to watch the souls depart and imagine them going up to God's glory to bask forever more, to be free of pain and sin. These days, I'm not so sure. Perhaps they just vanish and in the end we're all so much nothing.

There is a figure forming in the shadows under the trees. I've seen it before, though it seems more solid now than it ever has been. The shadows of the branches of the trees morph into arms and legs and a twisted torso, gaps of streetlight still creeping through. I watch as it forms. I wish I had my cane to lean on.

The darkness steps forward out of the shadows. Its surface is like oil. It's closer to human than I've seen it before but there's an unnatural lengthening of its limbs, a subtle wrongness to its motions.

It smiles the kind of cut-mouth smile a child draws, split from cheek to cheek. Droplets of darkness form on its upper lip and drip drip down, strings drawing its face together again.

I look down at the girl. She is more an outline now, features gone, but she's still worryingly opaque. The young always cling the most stubbornly to life. I suppose I can understand why it's harder for her to move on, there's so much of her left.

The shadow reaches the gate. It's locked, though the locks the council use aren't much use against the shadow man. He lifts one arm, one unconvincing hand, and knocks. The knocks have no sound, but I feel them running right through me and they make me shiver. I don't back down. I stand my ground.

He looks at me and he waves. It would be jaunty if his arms bent at the right places. He opens his mouth again and there's no sound, but I *know* he's asking to come in. I *know* he's promising it'll be quick, that it won't hurt, that all of this will be over. It's more tempting than it should be. His gaze locked on me, compelling me to crack. It would be easy to give in. To rest. My knees shake, the force of its gaze, its intent, is almost too much.

The last tendrils of the dead girl curl around my feet. I meet the place where his eyes should be. I don't say anything, but I'm sure he understands.

Then the girl is gone, her last strands curling in the breeze.

The shadow man waits. I think, perhaps, he'll try to come through anyway. Then he turns and stumbles back to the shadows, limbs falling away, leaving only dark puddles of footsteps and I'm alone, again.

I adjust my stance, pulling my pointed heels from the mud where they sank, and allow myself a minute to lean on the grave stone. It was worse this time, stronger. I don't know how much longer I'm going to be able to hold out.

I'd thought death would ease aches but my bones still creak as I make my way back to the oldest corner of the graveyard. The stones here are worn and covered with moss and lichen, their dead long forgotten.

A dog is a good guardian. Strong and brave, as needs must.

I sit back on my grave and I wait.

E.L. Thompson

BB and The Three Little Pigs

BB stood in the gateway to his new land, pleased with the agreement he had made. Being the runt of his litter, BB had been a small pup and bullied at school. Everyone knew how the old pig had tricked BB's grandfather with his brick house and cooking pot, the piglets never let BB forget.

Huffing and puffing BB made himself relax, he stopped remembering the bullies, bullies that hurt more than any outside bruises and Mr. Farmer trusted him to do his job.

Mr. Farmer had given the pack land; all they had to do was look after all Mr. Farmer's land. Protecting homes and food for so many of the smallest animals. The hogs and stags especially were starting to destroy areas of woodland and BB knew exactly which three little piggies he wanted to start with. But first he needed a trap.

BB approached his Alphas with the rising sun explaining what Mr. Farmer expected from the wolf pack suggesting they start by thinning the deer herd to show Mr. Farmer the pack were serious about their agreement. The next few weeks were filled with planning and hunting, BB was lucky his Alphas were wise and understood the need for caring for the woodland and protecting the deer population.

As he expected, when BB returned to the new pack-lands after weeks of hunting, he found three houses. One of straw, one of sticks and one of bricks, those pigs were so predictable it was almost funny.

Walking up to the straw house BB played his part,

'Little pig, little pig, let me come in.'

'Not by the hairs on my chinny chin chin.'

'Then I'll huff, and I'll puff, and I'll blow your house down.'

BB took a deep breath ready to blow the straw house down, when he heard the back door open and trotters scampering on the hard ground to the second house.

Smiling to himself, he stuffed his clothes with as much straw as he could and walked to the house made of sticks.

'Little pigs, little pigs, let me come in.'

'Not by the hairs on our chinny chin chins.'

'Then I'll huff, and I'll puff, and I'll blow your house down.'

BB didn't have time to take a breath before he heard a door open and trotters scratching to the stone house. Picking up as many of the sticks as he could carry, BB followed the pigs to the brick house. Before knocking on the door, BB went to the back and used some of his straw to block the gaps. Then used his sticks to jam the door shut. Happy with his work, BB knocked on the door, knowing this was going to be a very difficult job.

'Little pigs, little pigs, let me come in.'

'Not by the hairs on our chinny chin chins.'

'Then I'll huff, and I'll puff, and I'll blow your house in.'

So, BB huffed and puffed. He puffed and huffed. He puffed and puffed and huffed and huffed. Until he had no huff or puff left in him. BB sat for a rest and told the pigs he was going to climb down the chimney.

BB climbed to the top of the house and looked down, the chimney was dark and dirty, and BB could feel the heat starting to build from a fire below. These pigs really did do the same thing again because it worked once. Shaking his head in disbelief BB got back to work on his plan.

First he dropped the few sticks he had left to catch in the chimney Next he pulled out all the straw dropping some to catch on the sticks and packed the top of the chimney with the rest of it. Happy with his work BB climbed quietly down and waited.

Slowly the pack and many of the other animals came to see what was happening. Soon whole house was surrounded and still the pigs didn't come out, not all day or all night.

The next day Mr. Farmer came, and he found the three little pigs. The first one was stuck high in the chimney, smoked, trying to move the straw from his house. The second one was boiled when he fell into the pot trying to get the sticks from his house. The third piggy, well the third piggy built his house of bricks so it couldn't be blown away, but he still built his bed of straw right next to the fire, because it was soft and warm and easy to make. But straw is used for lots of things; it burns easily adding a wonderful flavour to your BBQ.

Hollie Glover

The King and The Stranger

The sun danced over the horizon, the city below sang with excitement. Sandstone buildings glowed, making their shadows deeper, their secrets darker. Across the city, people swarmed to taverns, dragging chairs from homes to enjoy the celebration of their King's birthday. Each party was so large, filling streets to the brim; they almost formed into one raging creature. Liquor poured freely. Barmaids drifted round streets giving anyone a drink, until they met one another, returning the way they came only to repeat the route all over again. The air hung heavy with the scent of food, family recipes, baked in the privacy of their homes before being presented to all in the streets. With each delicacy passed around, a scrutinising housewife followed, attempting to uncover the recipe of their competitors. After every bite, an approving hum followed.

Colourful banners and flags bearing the King's emblem of a panther flapped in the summer breeze. Flowers bloomed in every crevice of the city and Knights observed the ongoing festivities, dressed in their finest uniforms. Their gold breastplates glistened after being polished all night and their swords hung from their sides in new leather sheaths, concealing wooden blades inside.

The stranger drifted through the city, watching the people celebrate the glorious King. Before one of the many statues of their righteous leader, couples danced with energetic steps, rendering the stranger weary simply by observing. Women's skirts fluttered gracefully with each step and the men glided with such elegance they must have been deer in a past life. Little girls in their best, frilliest dresses attempted to mimic the steps, but ended up twirling chaotically, dizzying themselves. Round and round and round and...

Sitting at a tavern by the palace gate, the stranger was immediately greeted with a tankard of ale. Elder gentlemen told stories of the King they had heard from the elders before them at his birthday throughout their years. Hiding his bemused smile behind his tankard, the stranger listened to the stories, waiting for someone to claim the King had created fire.

'When the King first began his reign, hundreds of years ago, he...'

'We have not been at war since the King...'

'The outside world cannot taint us, as long as the wall and the King remain.'

His smile faltered. Suddenly, he could feel the King's eyes watching him. As if he knew an outsider was in his streets. The stranger peered up at the palace. White marble towers grasped for the sky, and darkened windows stared out at the world below.

Deep in the heart of the palace, the King paced his chambers. The sounds of his adoring citizens shook the windows, but it wouldn't help him smile. Instead he circled his room like a panther in a cage. Laying in his bed, her naked body hidden, was his wife. Her beautiful face, slightly damaged by the King's hand. Long, crimson hair. Blue, sparkling eyes. She watched the beast before her. In their one year of marriage, she had never seen him so nervous.

'What's wrong, my King?' she stuttered. His young face was taut with… she didn't know. Fear? But the King was never afraid. In his hand, he clutched a piece of parchment. He lay the message on his desk, and replied, 'Nothing.' The King stalked over to his bed. His reflection in the mirror paused him, he frowned at the copy of himself staring back. Reaching up to his hair, he plucked a grey strand from the rich, thick, gold nest atop his head. Held between two fingers, the single hair disintegrated into thin air. The King, forgetting the hair for a moment, continued to his wife. Her eyes had never left him. The King sat down on the bed and raised a hand to touch her face. She couldn't help but flinch. Still his hand stroked the small imperfection on his dear wife's face.

'My dear, I want to thank you. Over the last year, you have kept my bed warm and, like my wives before you, given me a beautiful child.' He wiped a tear from her cheek, before kissing the trail it had left behind. She went cold at the touch. Frost covering her soul. The kiss stopped. She could breathe again.

Once she regained her voice, she whispered, 'Happy birthday, your Majesty.' A sinister smile tugged at his lips, and he stood to leave. It was time to prepare for another new wife.

Abbi Peace

Autumn Anne

Every night I get home there's a naked body in my bed. I pray for each time to be the last. She lies there but doesn't move. Her chest slowly rises and falls with a rhythm I catch myself echoing. Her wide-open eyes circle manically round and round; this is exactly what I tried to avoid. They're desperate for a gaze to lock onto. I crinkle my eyes tight shut so it can't be me. In the darkness, I see how she used to be.

I remember when I met Anne because I'd been good that year. It was late September and it made the early evenings dark the way September does. It was two-hundred-and-seventy-one days since Emily and now I was beginning to heal. I thought I'd never look at another woman again, the way you always think when you lose one... until another comes along and gets under your skin. I was walking through the park, on my way home from church, when a small dog bounded seemingly out of nowhere at my ankles. I swung my leg back to boot the little bastard into next week, and then remembered that's what the old me would've done.

The next night was dark again. The trees loomed above me and cast the pathways into blackness. I could have just as easily had my eyes closed. Leaves were scattered beneath naked branches and were wet from rain and tramps' piss. Ahead, the paths met and opened out into a field which was brighter under the lamppost light. People were scattered about – doing people-in-park things. On one of the benches, at the edge of the field, sat Anne. She wasn't Anne to me then but she soon would be. I hated it when they had a name.

I wasn't sure how I'd never seen her before. Maybe she had just moved here, I thought; or maybe the Emily curse had just finally worn off. Anne was a wild garden. Her hair was red and rolled out from beneath her woolly hat. Her skin was milky and she smelt of burnt orange and cinnamon. She'd been sent to me. I never thought I'd be this lucky again, but there she was. I inhaled the air around her. That's as close as I'd let myself get.

My eyes creep open to the girl next to me in bed. Her hair is wet and knotted and there are leaves caught up in it. Her skin is wrinkled and damp. My angel is ugly and broken. A flower with no roots, ripped from Earth.

Every evening in church I'd say my thanks for Anne and then head to the park to see her again. Tonight was always going to be the last. Somehow, it never was. I'd walked that way anyway, even before I'd seen her, but Anne made the walks warm. She didn't look like Emily and I was glad. It would be too cruel to go through that again. I couldn't let myself. After all that'd happened, I knew better than to get involved with Anne but it didn't stop, that little niggle of hope to be close to someone again.

My stomach churns. I retch. Every time I see her lying there I want to vomit. It's just bile. I wipe away what's caught in the bristles on my chin and snap my eyes back into the dark.

I don't think I'd ever have progressed from my fantasies. There'd been enough hurt already. But Anne – well, Anne's dog – had sealed our fate. It'd been at my ankles again but this time Anne had come looking for it. She'd come where she shouldn't have, out of the light. Lovely little thing, I'd told her it was. Anne, she'd said greeting me; this was the moment when Anne became Anne instead of just the fantasy. She did smell like cinnamon and now I'd accepted my gift.

My heart, I remembered, was erratic. I grabbed Anne. I dragged her back into the trees and threw her onto the watery mud beneath us. If she'd screamed I'd have let her go. She lay there but she didn't move. I was over her and though her eyes were tight shut I knew she could feel me there. She started praying and it stopped me for a second. He wants you back, I told her. And I made it quick. I erased her face afterwards, and with care. She was less – Anne – then. Could've been anyone.

Yet she still visits me every night and I don't know how to make her go. Something is keeping her here and she is not where she's meant to be. I know I have forgiveness though, even if she's the one I can't forgive myself for. She was the light but I am the dark.

And she's ruined me.

Amy Craig

No, I Am Not

I am not the one who launched that plastic bottle into the sea. Penetrating the surface briefly, before emerging with a bob, to begin its journey out into the vast open plains of waters. When I saw him launch that bottle, I knew what person he was going to become. He looked about fourteen, and can't have been an avid news watcher, but who is? Maybe he is ignorant, or ill informed? Maybe he's expressing his masculinity to the girls in his wake? Not comprehending the damage his factory formed piece of plastic will cause, cutting its way through the ocean waves, waiting for its target.

No, I am not that boy, and nor will I be.

I am not the one with the bank card in my hand that does not possess my name. Staring gleefully down at what this could bring, placing it in my pocket without a thought of who this Mrs Debra O'Brien may be. I didn't invent a story for her. If she cared the card would already be stopped.

The bank will refund it anyway; it's my turn to have some damn fortune for a change. If it had happened to me, someone would do the same. People should be more careful. Fuck Debra O'Brien, she'll no doubt have four kids, two houses, a husband, and a lover she sees every Thursday, excusing her actions by saying 'I need some time for myself once in a while'. I'm glad I've found her card, she deserves to feel what it's like to have a thorn constantly pricked into your skin, reminding you of how unescapable your life has become.

No, I am not the one inventing stories of people I don't know.

I am not the girl who ran away from home when she was only fourteen, leaving distraught parents cowering by the phone, waiting for The Call. She returned a month later as if she'd never left, responding to their questions with a FUCK and a YOU! She waited for her parents to fall asleep before leaving again, her pockets and bag bustling to the brim. When she was seven her parents had told her that stealing was a sin, but the divine light had now abandoned her. She'd chosen a needle and the warm embrace of a boy whose name she didn't know. At seventeen, her face was splashed across the papers alongside the inscription – She used to be a lovely girl, a dedicated follower of the lord, with a bright future.

No, I am not the girl who chose to run away.

I am not the one who shouted at the woman with the veil on the bus. Attempting to pull it off her and tell her it wasn't allowed. I didn't scream into her terrified face, in a language which she hoped to learn, but was yet unable to speak. I am not the bystanders who watched by with the feeling in the pits of their stomachs that they should help but worried what would happen to themselves if they did. I am not the one who chose to film it on my phone; she'll get her retribution later, and watched as the tears ran down her face, pleading with her abuser to stop.

No, that was not me.

I am not the man who told his wife and kids he loved them; that he was sorry he had to work late again tonight. I didn't tell my kids I'd bring them something nice from my weekend trip away, only to realise at the services a mile away from home my broken promise. A Kit Kat each will do, sending them your apologies on return, I'll get something better next time, I promise. Kissing your wife on the cheek, it's been a long one, I better rest. Whilst you sleep blissfully, undisturbed by your broken promises, an unmoving pair of eyes has their aim set on the ceiling. She looks within herself the courage to fire, but each time firing a blank. Having no family, this cannot be me.

I am the one: the one who watches beyond the walls, the one who peers through the cracks and waits. Waits for you to make your repeated selfish mistakes. I watch in the darkened clouds of night as you lay curled in your sheets, remaining unperturbed. I am the one who offered you a chance to change, to think about your pain infesting ways, but you were blind. You ignored me, that feeling buried in your gut, that nagging thought tapping on your frontal lobes, and breathing down your neck.

I am the one who whistled in the waves,
clinging in the breeze,
waiting for you to change.

Andrew Milne

Love Letters

Dear Mrs Warren,

I am writing in response to your letter to the Board of Governors.

I understand you have been banned from the school premises for six months and would like to offer the following information:

18th May: You were not aware that your leggings had faded in the wash and were completely transparent. You assure us you would have worn pants if you knew this to be the case, or at least made an effort to shave.

6th September: You accused Esther's teacher, Mr Thompson, of inappropriately staring at your chest. It transpired that Mr Thompson was trying to read the writing on your t-shirt, that said Fuck Mondays. The reason he was staring for so long was because you had a substantial stain over some letters that impeded his reading. Apparently, you accidently dipped your left breast into a jug of gravy the evening before.

31st October: You dressed up as the clown from IT for the school Halloween disco. Four children cried when they saw you, as did two members of the PTA.

15th December: You instructed Esther to method-act her interpretation of a donkey for our Nativity, so she ate nothing but carrots for a week and would only go to the toilet on a bed of straw. In your letter, you state that Daniel Day-Lewis wouldn't be expected to just 'turn up and become a donkey' and accused our school of institutional sexism.

21st December: All staff members received a Christmas card from Esther that said: instead of presents this year, I am donating money to a charity that educates children about consent. Perhaps if God had known a bit more about the subject, Mary would have been famous for something other than giving birth in a barn to our boy JC. While we encourage children to express their opinions, I must remind you that we are a faith-based school. Esther needs to recognise that she is not in a position to teach God anything, especially since she refuses to learn her 7x table.

7th March: For World Book Day you dressed Esther as a vulva, claiming she was the protagonist from your self-published book, My

Vagina and Other Stories. Esther used a wet doll to mime the story of her birth.

1st April: In the most serious incident to date, you had a physical altercation with our Reception teacher. You claimed that Mrs Brown pulled your hair without provocation and you slapped her in retaliation. It transpires that you had six midget gems stuck in your ponytail and our sixty-two-year-old teacher was trying to help you.

Given the above actions, I will be upholding your ban from the school premises. If you feel you have further information that has not been considered, you are welcome to contact me via letter. Please do not come to the school again disguised as a postman, I will not discuss this with you in person while the ban is in place.

Kind regards, Mr Warren

Dear Mr Warren,

Thank you for your letter. I apologise for approaching you at school disguised as Postman Pat (I thought the fake cat was a give-away, but apparently not).

I respect your difficult position as the Chair of Governors and also my husband – it must make your job harder to have such an embarrassing wife. I'm hardly ever on time for drop-off and I flatly refuse to join the PTA. I never look presentable anymore; it is difficult to find appropriate clothes when your body resembles a pear dropped from height.

The truth is I don't think I was designed to be a mum. My body has not bounced back. I hate cooking, shopping, cleaning, ironing, hoovering. I dread 3:30pm. I love Esther but she can be a lot. Last week she cried for forty minutes because her imaginary friend wouldn't stop barking like a dog.

You know when I went away last month, to stay with my dad? That was a lie. I used the Child Benefit money and booked into a hotel. I napped on your side of the bed, ate an entire birthday cake and I farted without impediment. I had a lovely time.

Don't worry about lifting my ban from school, you are far better equipped for playground duties. I only appealed your decision so we could carry on writing to each other. It reminded me of our courting days in the beginning, when you lived away and we would send randy letters in the post. When we saw each other, we had sex with the lights on and spent hours reading and drinking wine. Do you remember that red one I used to like? Me neither.

3:20pm. Time to look busy.

Yours, Mrs Warren

Abby Knowles

Commotion in the Corporation

Though the arches maybe golden on the outside, on the inside they are rusting. Tattered seats are my main view for eight hours. My right hand is clenched to the till; it's the only thing keeping me from collapsing into a coma. I had too much fun last night, the bottle of wine still fresh in memory, the night itself forgotten. The vats create a nauseating smell. I rest my chin on my chest and pick up a straw. I begin to play with it in between my fingers. Working for the corporation isn't something I want to be doing, but the excessive drinking has brought me here.

Now I wonder, was it worth it?

I stay frozen, my mouth wide open causing drool to trickle out onto my arm. Two sticky, mucus thick lines now running down the hairy concourse to get to my fingers. 'Go left line go!' I think; intrigued by this fake race I created in my head. I lift my hand up from the counter and wipe away the drool on my uniform.

I was snapped into reality when the boss screamed my name 'Ben! There is a customer!' I rolled my eyes so hard I could feel my skull cracking and I turned to face the till. I raise my eyebrows and look up. I jolt back in surprise and take a step back. Well, who do we have here! It's him. The bastard. The bitch. The whore. I feel my sweat squeeze itself back into my skin to hide away from this monster. With my lips and teeth chattering, I take the order:

'What would you like to order sir?'(Though, you're more a rodent).

'I'll have a burger, no pickle, extra cheese and a dollop of mayonnaise!' (Awkward bastard)

'Sure... and what drink would you like today?' (Probably something cold like his heart)

'Just a bottle of water, I don't drink unhealthy things.' (But you're in McDonald's again)

'Anything else you would like today?' (Perhaps a slap?)

'No thank you... and this is to go, the atmosphere here is rather drab.' (Just like your personality then)

'So that's £4.99, there is a wait due to your order, I hope that's okay.' (Tough shit if it isn't)

'I guess so.' (You guess so, it's a simple yes or no answer...)

I turn my back and roll my eyes once more, I can see the veins of my brain showering my eye sockets from the thing it just saw. I blink back into reality and waves of whining crash into my ears like a tsunami. Could it be the screams of a toddler, or the moans of the old woman who goes off on one when she only gets two sticks of milk? No, it's much worse; it's the bleeping of the fry vats.

They moan when they need filtering, when they need fresh oil, when the fries need shaking and when they are cooked. They never shut up. With every cry, they bellow, I feel my brain cramp tighter.

The beep starts again, a siren for the frozen artificial potato sticks as they are dropped into the bubbling oil for human consumption. Very few escape onto the floor but they are trampled on and brushed away into the dustbins.

'Will you actually shut up' I thought as I filled up the medium and large fry boxes up to minimum levels. I take a portion of fries to the bag and I lay them just so that they will all fall out of the box.

With the fries placed it was time to see if the order was ready – with the thing having an awkward order we've got a wait for a fresh batch of 10:1 meat to be cooked and for it to be dressed before it's placed in the production bin. No, it's not actually a bin. We're not that unhygienic (though our secret seasoning is rubbing the crown of the bun on the floor).

It's been 67 seconds and the order is still not ready. At this moment I should be taking more orders, but with my head still banging, that was never going to happen. 'Minimum wage, minimum effort' I said to myself, and I crept along to the fridge to grab a bottle of water.

I take the water and I misplace my hand, a gushing sound of twenty water bottles fall out of the fridge all over the floor. My face blends red like a sand storm that covers my slate skin. 'For fuck sake!' Again, I think, 'minimum wage, minimum effort' and kick the bottles to the side. As I'm doing so, I see the thing's order in the production bin. 'Oh, thank God!' I sprint over and grab the burger. I place it into the bag and lift it up.

'There you go, have a nice day.' (Go get hit by a bus)

Ben Ambrazaitis

Gunshot

Officer Ramona Carlisle held her gun with confidence. Aiming it at the six foot four, Caucasian male. Estimated to be thirty-eight and easily out weighing her. She knew firing her weapon was a last resort, and she hated the very idea of using it but she also knew that criminals like this could smell hesitation and fear, both of which she refused to exhibit signs of. She could shoot and kill if she needed it, especially for the sake of the petrified ten-year-old girl that was currently being held hostage. The situation was an extremely delicate one. Carlisle had been forced to go in alone in the hopes of distracting the offender long enough for backup to arrive before she had a dead girl on her hands. The grimy abandoned warehouse was not where Ramona wanted anyone to die, especially, and a little selfishly, her. Flicking her eyes to check her watch she could feel panic rising in her throat. Where was her backup? When she'd called it in the ETA had been five minutes, but that must have been ages ago. What was going on? She'd never been let down before and the fear was slowly seeping in. As if he could tell, the criminal swung his gun towards Ramona, waving it and screaming unintelligibly. Things were spiralling quickly out of her control and the situation would soon escalate to become much worse, she knew for certain. Then she heard the loud crack of the door downstairs and knew her backup had arrived. She watched as the man's eyes went wide, his gun still trained on Ramona, hers on him. No, this wasn't right. The fear was making him angrier. Suddenly they both raised their guns to point at each other's foreheads.

The gunshot echoed through the warehouse.

Stacy Curry

String Making

I can still remember getting my 'funny' string. Being awarded it. At seven years old, I'd started a new school, left on the playground by my mum who gave me a pat on the head and told me to go make friends. Not an ounce of worry in her voice. Lipstick smile a red smear across her face. Glossy and immaculate. Her 'perfectionist' string shining strong.

After a brief assessment of my surroundings, I'd selected a target. A girl sitting alone on a bench, book in hand, twin pigtails swaying in the morning breeze. No one sat near her, or even looked her way. Bounding over, I'd beamed, braid swinging side to side over my spine.

I'd sat down beside her. Not knowing then that she was to become my best friend, to give me another one of my strings – 'Josie's best friend'. One that is still with me today. Strong as ever.

Josie had looked at me, half closing the book and lowering it to her lap. I had smiled; then offered up my strings. Back then, I didn't have many. Like all of us at that age, I defined myself through my childish pleasures.

At the time, Pocahontas was my favourite Disney character. She looked like me and I thought her raccoon was cute. So I'd taken her as a string. I had 'swimmer' too, from all the lessons my dad sent me to. My favourite colour had been orange – very important – so that was the first thing I'd told Josie. As a form of introduction. Brashly pulling the 'orange' string forward for her to see, offering that first part of myself.

She'd glanced up at it long enough to feel the meaning, tentative eyes trailing upwards along the string I'd revealed. Then she'd offered me her own. Tiny fingers plucking, guiding it forward. I'd looked up at its tip, floating inches above her head, and felt the answer. Her favourite colour was green.

I'd joked that together we made a carrot. And she'd laughed. More than I had expected – her girlish trill ruptured the air, high and clear. It coaxed a grin from me, and then I'd felt it. The birth of a new string. The way it wrapped around something in my chest and tightened as I settled into it. 'Funny'.

I'd pushed it then, testing, pulling the string to gauge its strength.

Another comment had Josie laughing again. In response, the string went pleasantly taut, tugging gently on a single rib-bone as my 'funny' string floated forwards of its own accord, presenting itself.

Glowing in the aftermath of this new addition to my collection, I'd gazed above Josie's head, eyeing the other string tips I could see there. But as with everyone new, they were blurred, moving too hastily to see until she herself showed me. Until she wanted me to see more of who she was.

I learned them all over the years. Even gave her some new ones.

An 'Elena's best friend' string appeared to match my own. And my eleven-year-old-self dubbed her a 'Hufflepuff' before I'd even convinced her to read Harry Potter.

I myself kept a firm grasp on my 'Gryffindor' string in those early days of our friendship. It had seemed to fit nicely with my others. I had one for 'bold', one for 'loud', and one bestowed by my mum from a very young age. 'Little madam', she'd titled me, using it whenever I was cheeky or rolled my eyes at her. But I'd liked the sound of it. Had pictured myself trotting down the street in her clacking heels and oversized work blazer, my mouth coated in her lipstick. A true little madam. So I'd taken it with pride. I even gained a pair of strings – 'scary' from my other classmates, and 'a handful' courtesy of my teachers – after I pushed Sam Roits for trying to give Josie a 'weirdo' string. He'd banged his head and cut his lip. But I didn't care. I'd have cut the string myself if he'd managed to force it on Josie. All very 'Gryffindor' in my eyes.

I'd relinquished it as I grew older, though. Starting secondary school taught me that I was more of a 'Ravenclaw'. So, I'd untied it with a sad smile, and let it drift away.

That wasn't the only string I'd freed for the sake of another. I'd had 'mathematician' when my dad realised I was excellent at maths. He'd wanted me to become an accountant. But then I discovered French. Learnt that I loved languages, learnt that I loved the feel of foreign words dancing on my tongue, learnt that I wanted nothing to do with a future in numbers. I'd happily cut the 'mathematician' string that day.

But 'funny', that was mine forever.

Jamie-Louise Shakeshaft

Mr Smith

Mr Smith comes into the restaurant every Saturday night at 8pm. He eats six oysters in the bar; the staff don't offer him Tabasco, even though it is customary. He orders a bottle of Pinotage; a rich, deep red wine, and one glass. The waitress takes him to his table, a table he sits at every week. It is set up for one. The waitress doesn't offer him water, even though it is customary. For starter, he has the mussels, and for main course, half a steak and half a lobster. The waitress doesn't bring him the free vegetables, even though it is customary. His meal isn't on the menu, but the chefs do it anyway. The waitress doesn't offer him coffee or dessert, even though it is customary. Mr Smith doesn't ask for the cap for his wine, but the waitress brings it anyway because she knows he only drinks half the bottle. As he pays the bill the manager books him in for dinner next week, at 8pm.

Tonight, Mr Smith is being served by the new waitress. She offers him Tabasco, he smiles and says no. She asks what wine he wants, but the bar man is already bringing the Pinotage over; the new waitress blushes and walks away embarrassed. She sits him at the wrong table in the restaurant, but he doesn't say anything. She's forgotten to take away the other table setting so the table is set for two; in an awkward hurry she removes the other setting while Mr Smith watches. She offers him water, which he declines, and takes his order. She tells Mr Smith she will have to ask the chefs if the lobster and steak combination is alright. He smiles politely and says, 'I'm sure it'll be fine dear'. She brings out the free vegetables with his dinner and he leaves them off his plate. Afterwards, she offers him coffee and dessert, he declines. He asks for the cap for his wine, pays his bill and leaves. The new waitress doesn't book him in for next week at 8pm.

Mr Smith has been coming to the restaurant for twenty-five years and for the last eight he has been coming alone. Twenty-five years ago, he came in with his wife: every Saturday, at 8pm. They would have a bottle of Pinotage and twelve oysters, Mrs Smith would have Tabasco on hers. They sat on the same table every week, a table for two by the window. She had water but he never did. They would both have mussels for starter and for their main course she would order lobster and he would order the steak. They would split their dishes and eat half of each; Mrs Smith would eat the vegetables. She would have a dessert afterwards and give him a spoonful while he finished the bottle of wine. They would pay the bill and the manager would book them in for next week at 8pm.

Vicky Booth

Death in New Orleans

'I looked, and behold, an ashen horse: and he who sat on it had the name Death: and Hades was following with him.' Death sighs – a deep, melancholic sigh – and closes the cover, tossing the book to the ground. 'Well, that's some bull.'

Death's having a bad day. He's on strike.

He sits in an empty graveyard, huddled against the tomb of one John Pullman. It's a small tomb; basic, cheap. John didn't amount to much – Death can relate. The wispy grey souls orbiting his head come closer, chittering and nagging. They pull at the hood of his cloak and tap against his bare skull.

'Yes, yes. I know.' He swats them away, pulling the hood closer around his face. 'I'm sure you're just *dying* to get down there, but I need a break. Over two thousand years of work and not one single day off. Centuries of toil and grind, constant whining and begging. Do you know how tiring that gets? No one ever asks me what I want! "Hey Death, what do you want from life?". But no, I haven't even lived.'

Beep beep. Death raises his skeletal wrist, the smartwatch's lighted screen too bright for his eye sockets. *Reminder: collection date* – he slams the snooze button, revealing a rather charming background of Margaret Thatcher.

'Not today, Satan, not today,' He grumbles. 'I am Death; reaper of souls, destroyer of worlds… Nah, I don't even know what I want. It's a hard life when you're the most loathed concept around… a bit of appreciation would be nice. Wouldn't it, Johnny boy?' He chuckles and elbows the tomb playfully.

'Who you talking to, bro?' Death looks up to find a figure leaning against another tomb. He's small, pale and impossibly thin with a bargain bucket of chicken wings tucked under one arm: Famine. He shoves another wing into his mouth as he speaks; 'You better not be going crazy again you know what happened last time, when you and Pestilence tag teamed Europe… I'm talking about the plague.'

'Ugh, how did you find me?' Famine pushes off the wall and shuffles over to Death. He crouches down and offers the bucket.

'It wasn't hard. Wing?' He gestures at the surroundings and Death gasps in horror.

'Could you be any more insensitive? You know poor John here choked to death on a chicken wing.' Death spreads his arms across the tomb walls, as if to hide the bucket from its sight. 'Don't look, Johnny… and you *know* I'm vegetarian. So, where's the rest of the Brady Bunch?'

'Vegetarian? Alright, PETA.' He reaches out a bony hand to pat Death on the shoulder. 'We're worried about you, it's been three days since you last collected any souls and it's getting a bit out of hand. You can't mope in New Orleans forever.'

Death shrugs off his brother's hand and rises to his feet, grabbing his scythe from the ground. With a sigh, Famine also stands – placing the bucket on a gravestone – and moves to the tomb opposite John's.

'So, they sent you to try and convince me to come back. Well I won't do it, and you can't make me. I'm my own… Death, and I'm going to go and find my true self.'

'Come on, buddy, why don't we speak to the Old Man first?'

The tomb doors open with a *ping* revealing a dingy elevator, the screams of hell only just muffled by the music. Stood by the doors is Charon, the ferryman of the dead, in an ill-fitting bell hop uniform. Famine tosses a gold coin which he fumbles to catch.

'Going down?'

Megan Tait-Davies

Bitter

Two John Smith's please, pal. God, I've been craving this pint.

I turn to Tom, an anticipatory smile plastered on my face. It's his round, and he knows it's his round. What hangs in the balance here is whether he's actually gonna get it. As is the time-honoured tradition in this country of beer drinkers, you always pay your way. We're all as skint as the next fella. Get your round in.

After several seconds of he and I mentally shooting laser beams at each other, he eventually sighs and whips his faded Yorkshire Bank card out. *Contactless, please.*

It's just after seven in the evening. A dark, chilly night in York. Not that we're griping. We've got a nice little oak table for two by a log fire. Our shelter of choice is the Red Lion. My drinking buddy is an old student friend, Tom. While I've stayed for the long run and started an MA, he's on an engineering traineeship in Bradford.

We're commemorating our current state of affairs down my local.

Once we've taken that inaugural sup, I start shooting the shit. *How's the course going, then?*

Tom shakes his head and takes an extended gulp. *Shite, to be perfectly honest.*

Why?

He takes a deep breath. *You know that Ben lad I mentioned last week?*

Bastard Ben? From Carlisle?

Yeah. Well, he had a go at me this morning.

How come?

I was chatting to Jen in the workshop about having to move house because of our landlady dying. Out of nowhere, Ben turns around and starts calling me a 'spoiled brat who's had it easy'. Saying I've 'never known true struggle'. He's not telling Jennifer this, who has a solicitor dad and a semi-detached in Haworth. No, it's me, the lad with two grand of overdraft debt without as much as a pot to piss in.

It's not you though is it? It's him. If you've done nowt to him, there's no reason he'd dislike you that much. I can see in Tom's eyes that he has, in fact, done something.

Well, I did call him a smackhead when were out in Shipley that time.

Of course. *Okay. Well, he's probably just been touchy over that. What was your response to all this anyway?*

Well, as you know, I'm pretty laid-back at the worst of times. But I couldn't be on with this. Some 'rehabilitated' junkie telling me that just because I haven't had to sleep in a shop doorway I've had it easy? I wasn't fucking having it, Pat.

I look down at my trainers. From many past occasions, I've learnt that Tom is no Tony Robbins. He doesn't handle well under pressure. I take a long sip of beer to prepare myself for the embarrassing comeback he'd given.

So?

I smacked him.

I let out a high-pitched laugh. *Oh well, you sorted that perfectly.*

He stares at me like a dog that's just shat on the kitchen floor. *I got caught up in the moment.*

Tyson Fury over here. Did he fight back?

Did he fuck. He was lying in the foetal position, the shitbag. I still said sorry, like. Graham, my instructor, sent me home and told me they'd have to hold a disciplinary hearing.

I sigh like a disappointed Dad. *Fuck's sake, man.*

I'm gonna end up on the Dole again, I just know it. I'll be lucky if he doesn't press charges, to be honest.

There's not a chance he'll go the police. They'll most likely keep you on, just so long as you play your cards right.

Tom sneers and takes another lengthy sip. *If they don't, fuck 'em. Course is full of losers anyway.*

I look to the side, as if to an invisible camera. Alas, it's just the two of us trapped inside this bubble of cheap ale and self-sabotage.

Tom is clearly eager to change the subject; without a word, I let him.

So how's you and Patti Smith doing?

This makes me chuckle with a mouthful of beer. *Jade?*

Couldn't even remember her name, yeah.

We both laugh obnoxiously, just enough to take the edge off for a moment. I swallow down my mouthful of drink. *We're not speaking.*

Oh, what? Why?

I just caught really bad vibes from her.

You always do this. You never go by any actual evidence that your

*relationship's on its arse. You just smell something in the air and fuck off
if it isn't roses.*

    I go by instinct, which is better than anything.

    Tom smiles wryly and shakes his head. *What is it with me and you?*

    How should I know?

    I think the cosmos just isn't in our favour.

    We finish our pints and head to the bar for another round.

Patrick Morgan

The Man Who Smiled

The sky promised rain. She stepped outside and was buffeted by a gripping breeze. Noises contended unseen around her; chirping birds, a neighbour beating dust from a rug, the distant rumble of a motor, and a noise any other person might have missed, but not Jean. The soft, long-suffering whisper of her father sanding wood in the shed. The sound made Jean pause; a surge of emotion lifting in her throat.

She drew a deep breath and tasted the rich afternoon; the garden slowly awakening after a season of slumber, the heady sting of varnish and paint leaking from the open shed, and her aromatic, floral perfume which her father said gave colour to his days. Knowing that, she applied it generously.

She walked down the path, her hand trailing along the metal rail. The sanding ceased abruptly; he had heard her approach or had caught a whiff of her scent. His distinguished voice, a deep baritone, ushered her inside. 'Jean, sweetheart.' His smile was the first thing she saw, passing under the doorframe. 'Can you hear the birds? They must be out building their nests.'

'Yes, before the rain. Tea is almost ready, have you finished here?'

'Rain, dear?'

'Yes, the sky's growing dark.'

George angled his head, as if listening for something just out of hearing. On his face was a frown that didn't belong. It was then that Jean's eyes were drawn to the gaping cavity on her father's brow, above his right eye. The graft of thick, sunken skin bridging the horrific expanse seemed to be the only thing preventing her from tumbling straight through into the dark landscape of his mind.

Purposefully, she focused on her engagement ring, and the account of her mother's wedding sprung to mind. Father was away fighting in the Second World War, mother at home making all the preparations. Then the telegram arrived with the seal of the British Army. Mother sunk to her knees. She had already hired the dress, the trestles, the chapel. The neighbours had baked the cake. The paper trembled in her hands as she read father's leave had been nulled. The air left her in swift, shuddering exhalations. Weeks later, without any warning, father was granted a weekend off. In great spontaneity they were married the same day, with no flowers, cake, or trimmings, and a borrowed dress. Over the coming months father visited sporadically, coming and going without time to breathe. He received a letter that mother was pregnant before the year was through.

George later told his daughter that, as he read the words back, tears of sheer wonderment had filled his eyes.

She didn't know if he ever thought back to the day he stepped out into the firing range with his head held high, galvanised by the news. He would have wheeled to face his battalion, seeing extra colours rising through the morning, as if to herald the shifting lanes of his future. But did he see the bullet ricochet from a tree and lance into his forehead? In her mind, Jean saw the bullet strike the trunk, saw it bounce off in a welter of bark, saw it rock his head backwards. She lived the scene every time she laid eyes on the wound that stole all the colours from his world.

The silence in the garden shed was interrupted by the mechanical thunder of an approaching train and the low flight of a starling across the open doorway. George looked up, a smile chasing the shadows from his countenance. He kept track of the time by listening for the trains.

He indicated his work. 'Tell me, what do you think?' He was making another narrow, cradle-like stand which would hold a row of plant pots. 'This one's for Auntie Rose.'

'It's splendid. She'll love it.'

'I'll paint it tomorrow. Come on, let's not keep your mother waiting.' He swivelled from his stool and took Jean's hand. His skin was rough, hardened from years of carpentry, and she winced slightly in his solid grip.

They stepped outside, and the dipping light washed over his features. Jean glimpsed the scar, saw the bullet strike the bark and rebound with a metallic flash. Tenderly she guided him to the rail. 'You should really have your stick with you.'

'I'm fine, dear,' he said, taking hold of the metal pole. As they crossed the garden he began to hum.

Jean pondered the many ways to identify this man. Husband, father, uncle. The war general with the soothing voice. The man with a hole in his head. A sightless man.

But to her he was the man who always sought the positives. It turns out you don't need eyes for that. For all he had seen, and all he had not, he was the man who always smiled.

Gas Leak

Shadows lengthen in the fading light, following the man as he makes his way down the trail into the woods. Silhouetted trees hide the animals who hold their breath as the man passes by, not daring to make a sound. The crunching of leaves beneath his heavy boots echoes around the surrounding trees. His breath forms clouds of white in front of him. Shivers run down his spine and he hunches his shoulders to protect himself from the harsh wind. His unruly, brown hair (he should have cut it weeks ago) is whipped away from his face and, for a moment, he is no longer anonymous.

No one knows him around here; he wants to keep it that way.

Hands in his pockets he picks up his pace ever so slightly, now almost halfway home thanks to the shortcut through the woods. He can no longer see the roads lining either side. A twig snaps, shattering the silence. Slowly, he turns, unable to see anything but leering shadows. It is already much darker than when he had first entered the woods. Dusk has finally settled under the treetops. The hairs rise on the back of his neck, goose-bumps race up his arms. He continues down the trail. After a few minutes, he shakes his head and chuckles under his breath trying, and failing, to rid himself of the feeling that he is not alone. He tells himself he's just paranoid before taking a deep, calming breath. Just paranoid.

He coughs, the air is thick with smoke, it settles on his tongue like a thick vinegary wine. He looks up in bewilderment at the plumes of grey rising through the saplings a little way off. He follows the track of smoke with his eyes, then takes off at a run, lungs burning with the inhalation of each slow, polluted breath. Ahead, he sees the tree line and, beyond it, firefighters attempting to contain a fire. And then the realisation hits. His house is burning. He tries to run forward but stops. He can't go any further. He can't be seen. On instinct he reaches for the old, worn, metal box in his inner breast pocket. He stares in silence as he recalls the snapping of the twig. The sensation of being followed. It had not been paranoia. They were already here. It dawns on him as he feels the icy metal against the rough flesh of his fingers. He can't let them have it. But his home… burnt down.

They already knew it wasn't there.

Without thinking he takes off at a sprint and is soon clear of the woods. It was not his paranoia. They were here. Running along the edge of the tree line he keeps to the shadows, away from prying eyes. Breathless, he hunches over at the side of the road. By now she will have seen the fire, understood what it meant. It had been drilled into them both – where to meet, what to do, how to stay safe. Hidden, he waits for her. Barely used, the bus stop was the best place to meet if they ever needed a way out (or at least that's what they had been told). He hears the rumbling of two engines approaching and retreats further into the shadows. Unable to see either of the driver's faces through the windscreens, he continues to wait. No doubt they know he is here. Something is wrong, he doesn't exactly understand what, but something isn't right. Having never seen the woman he was meant to be meeting face to face, he didn't know what to look for. He'd only ever had phone conversations with her and written letter correspondence. It was safer that way. Once again, the hairs on the back of his neck rise and goose-bumps race along his arms. Taking another step back towards the trees, he feels the cold metal of a gun pressing into his skull.

News report from *The Daily News*, March 18, 2014:

COUPLE FOUND DEAD IN WOODS AFTER HOUSE FIRE
The bodies of a man and woman have been found in the woods by Oakwood Road. The man has been identified by police as Peter Dowell, whose house caught fire only hours before the bodies were discovered by a member of the public. The police have refused to comment on whether any foul play has taken place. The woman is yet to be identified.

Grace Morris

Four Ghosts of Martin Croft

1.

The pavement had a name, or at least the slab did; Martin Croft. There were two of them. The son lived only to fifteen weeks, the father to sixty-nine years. He died in 1800.

A name is already a fiction, already a story. The surname tells of ancestors, gives a history that stretches back before birth. And what is encoded in the forename? Martin, derived from the god of war. Did his parents mean him to be aggressive; did he live up to it? I had only a name, but I was already inventing him.

I took his identity. My Martin would be fifteen, on the verge of his adulthood. I made the dead child a younger brother instead of a son, who never reached his first birthday; a tragic detail that would arouse sympathy for my new character. The slab also told of a wife, Ann; I had no use for her so I left him unmarried.

I learnt about my characters even as I created them, discovering rather than inventing their life stories. It amused me to make my fifteen-year-old Martin a writer; I even composed stories for him, all displaying a yearning to succeed but no true ability. None were finished; some of them even trailed off mid-sentence.

Should I feel guilty at taking Martin Croft's name like this? He wasn't using it any more. No one really knew of the man whose name, if not his body, was buried in the square. I, at least, rehearsed the name, bringing him back into being. His name was his ghost, and I would send it out into the world, to haunt and deceive.

I wondered what he'd think of me.

2.

I hate you. You stole my name, and made a ghost of me.

I watch you writing, immobile behind you. You don't know I'm here.

There was a real Martin, but I am not he. I do not remember his wife, nor his son. I had only a brother. And my stories.

I could have been a success, had I lived longer. I have known this ever since I found myself standing on my own memorial stone, invisible and inaudible to the passers-by. The stone beneath me was the only clue to my name. How had I become a ghost of Martin Croft?

I could forgive you the theft of my name. But you took my wife from me. I looked down at Ann's name on the slab and knew that you had neglected to create me a bride.

I remembered writing a story of my own creation; a short passage in which you took my name and built me a life founded on lies. The story was unfinished. I must finish it now.

I stand behind you, watching the back of your head as you type. Inside that head are all the details of my life that you invented, all those false memories of a man who never was. You are the ghost of Martin Croft, not me.

I raise my hand into the air, and bring it down upon.

3.

He set his quill down. Perhaps it was as well to leave it in mid-sentence. It amused him to write such fantasies, but the story was a failure.

He knew that literary success would elude him. There would be no memorial stone to him in the future. He hoped he would reach the sixty-nine years he had just given himself; he prayed more fervently that any future son would live longer than fifteen weeks. It had been truly evil to think that. He felt that imagining it had cursed it into being.

As for a wife, he despaired. He was still only in his fifteenth year, but he was too shy of the opposite sex. His Ann remained as much a fantasy as the rest of his ramblings.

Sometimes he felt like his own ghost. As if he flitted through life but had no effect on the outside world.

He wrote at the bottom of the page. 'Written in jest, this twelfth day of October, seventeen hundred and forty-six.'

He paused before signing his name. If names are the beginnings of stories, what fictions do we tell about ourselves with our own names?

He sighed, put the pen to paper again. 'Martin Croft,' he wrote. Then he left his desk.

'MARTIN, the son of Martin and Ann Croft, died the 8th day of March 1797, aged 15 weeks.

MARTIN CROFT, father of the above, died 10th of February 1800. Aged 69. […]

Also the said Ann Croft, who died 12th December 1833 in the 81st year of her Age, widow of the last named Martin Croft.'

[Memorial stone, King's Place, York.]

Neil James Hudson

Heat Death

A man is staring at his cat in the pink palace. His eyelids bare the weight of a thousand galaxies, yet still he pushes on. Still he continues to be. The cat meets his owner's eyes. His expression, were it worn by a human, would be one of pure contempt. The man asks, 'What are you so happy about?'

A pause. Silence floods the room. For a moment, the world feels wrong. Neither being appears to notice that the pink walls grow a shade darker.

The silence breaks, and the world returns to normal. 'I was being sarcastic.' The man admits. The cat seeks to correct the man. 'This is happy.' He thinks, gesturing toward himself.

I wonder if the man could hear that thought. Sometimes I catch a glimpse of myself in the mirror before I depart for work, I think about the cat's expression in this eternal dialogue. I see how close it is to my own, and I want to believe that this is happy.

John Liddle

Black Shuck

East Anglia doesn't have a lot of folklore. At least, not that I'm well aware of. We call ladybugs "Bishy-barnabys", but I don't think that counts. One that I do know is Black Shuck. "Shuck", meaning fiend or devil, "Black" meaning black. Black Shuck takes the form of – let's not mince words – a really big dog. A *really* big dog. Sometimes as big as a horse. The Darkness wrote a song about it. So whether Shuck is *the* devil, or just *a* devil, or just some kind of demon, the thing's bad news. It's a black dog, did I mention that? Kind of obvious, but that's folklore for you. Comes out at night, so you don't see the thing coming 'til it's too late, if you happen to be cycling into town because you've forgotten to get milk from the co-op and the old church comes up on your left and also, incidentally, there's ice on every outdoor surface in the country right now and you slide sideways into the gate *somehow* and down you go…

The Dog is no stranger to churches. In the 16th century it allegedly broke down the doors of the church in Bungay (Bun-GEE, with a hard G like in Goth or Grandma, or Goth Grandma) and killed two people. Wrung their necks, which strikes me as odd for a dog to do. So the Dog has A: incredible strength and B: presumably thumbs. That's fun. No way you could get away with that nowadays, people are too cynical. So that's a black dog, a *big* black dog possibly with thumbs, glaring at you as it stalks through the ancient headstones, names barely readable under the rot of time, in the cold darkness of a winter's night, when the birds are asleep and the insects have frozen solid and the only thing you can hear is that thing *breathing*…

One more fun thing about Black Shuck. If you see him, you'll be dead within the year.

So I've got that to look forward to.

Charles Plumb

Eric's Flat

Eric sat back in his chair and laughed. It was a passionless laugh. Unconcerned, uninvolved and unmoved.

What had the world come to?

He had been alone for five days now in total. Five days. Nearly all the fresh food had turned bad. The kitchen was filled with a rotten stench that left Eric gasping for clean air.

The lady from the home delivery team hadn't been in eight days. She was meant to come on Tuesday, that was three days ago. Soon all he would have left would be those shitty cans of soup his daughter brought him before Christmas.

'In case of an emergency' she'd said.

What emergency? Something like this perhaps?

Somehow, he didn't think that this is what she had in mind.

Looking out from his window, Eric could see no sign of light. No lights for five days.

'Something is definitely up with the world' he murmured.

On the first day Eric hadn't been particularly bothered.

Some-one will fix 'em soon, he thought to himself. *The world will be back to normal soon enough, the world always returns to normal eventually...*

But by the third day he had started to panic.

'There's no use in panicking though is there? What's that gonna do for you?' He asked himself.

With the fifth day drawing to a close, Eric felt nothing but a remarkable sense of calm. He had taken to staring out his window onto the street below. But thirteen stories up, he could barely make anything out of the gloomy mist that had enveloped the city. Sometimes he thought he could see people. They looked to be carrying bags or pulling suitcases. If they were leaving then there must be a reason. Eric didn't like to dwell on what that reason might be.

Anyway, what could he do?

He was up here. Trapped in a flat. Thirteen stories up. The only thing he could do was wait. With a sigh, Eric wheeled himself into the kitchen, opened a cupboard and pulled out a tin of soup...

Jessica Wright

Acknowledgements

Thank you to all the writers, artists and designers who submitted work to be used within this anthology. Each piece we saw was wonderfully crafted and we hope that their publication here is the springboard into new writing opportunities. We would also like to thank Jamie McGarry at Valley Press and the staff at York Centre for Writing who assisted with this publication.

www.ingramcontent.com/pod-product-compliance
Lightning Source LLC
Chambersburg PA
CBHW060355180626
46817CB00008B/3027